12/12

MAY

e share your thoughts c

LESSON OF THE
WHITE EAGLE

A NOVEL

BARBARA HAY

THE ROADRUNNER PRESS
OKLAHOMA CITY

Published by The RoadRunner Press
Oklahoma City
www.TheRoadRunnerPress.com

First edition hardcover, The RoadRunner Press, October 2011
Printed in the United States of America.
Illustrations by Peter Hay.
Map by Walker Creative, Inc.
Cover design by Jeanne Devlin.

This is a work of fiction. While the literary perceptions and insights
are based on experience, all names, characters, places, and incidents are
either products of the author's imagination or are used fictitiously.
No reference to any real person is intended or should be inferred.

Published October 12, 2011

Library of Congress Control Number: 2011925087

Publisher's Cataloging-in-Publication

(Provided by Quality Books, Inc.)

Hay, Barbara.
    Lesson of the white eagle : (a young adult novel) / Barbara Hay. — 1st ed.
    p. cm.
    SUMMARY: A boy questions his friends' attitudes toward Indians after
    the white eagle takes him back to see the forced removal of the Ponca to
    Oklahoma.
    Audience: Ages 12-18.
    LCCN 2011925087
    ISBN-13: 978-1-937054-00-7

    1. Indians of North America—Oklahoma—History—
Juvenile fiction. 2. Race relations—Oklahoma—Juvenile
fiction. 3. Ponca Tribe of Indians of Oklahoma—
Juvenile fiction. [1. Indians of North America—Fiction.
2. Race relations—Fiction. 3. Ponca Tribe of Indians
of Oklahoma—Fiction. 4. Oklahoma—History—Fiction.]
I. Title.

PZ7.H31382Les 2011   [Fic]

                        QBI11-600088

For my husband, Ron

"WHEN YOU ARE IN DOUBT, BE STILL, AND WAIT;
WHEN DOUBT NO LONGER EXISTS FOR YOU,
THEN GO FORWARD WITH COURAGE.

SO LONG AS MISTS ENVELOP YOU, BE STILL;
BE STILL UNTIL THE SUNLIGHT POURS THROUGH
AND DISPELS THE MISTS—AS IT SURELY WILL.

THEN ACT WITH COURAGE.

—WHITE EAGLE,
CHIEF OF THE PONCA

LESSON OF THE WHITE EAGLE

ONE

I OPENED MY LOCKER and tossed in my notebook. The sound of someone stomping on a fat tube of toothpaste, or worse, filled the air. I glanced left and right to see if anyone had heard, just as I remembered the banana I'd brought for lunch Monday but never eaten. I picked my book back up—afraid to look at what I knew was going to be ugly: Black peel hung off the cover; slime oozed from the broken seams of the banana. I dropped the book back in my locker in disgust.

Luckily it was Friday—even rotting banana couldn't get me down today.

Swarms of kids spilled from nearby classrooms, and the air buzzed with a contagious excitement as their voices passed me in the hall. Someone slapped me on the back, but before I could turn to see who it was, the culprit had slipped into the crowd filling the corridor. I turned back to my locker and caught my reflection in the mirror taped to the inside of the door. I cringed. I was letting my hair grow out from a summer buzz cut, and it wasn't going well.

I slicked down a few tufts of short black hair on the crown of my head, hoping that this time they might stay put; I grabbed a ball cap from my locker just in case they didn't, along with my blue-and-white Wildcats jacket, and headed for home.

All weekends are good, but this weekend promised to be historic. Our town was celebrating the centennial of the land run that created Ponca City back on September 16, 1893. Most of the families around here staked their claim for a piece of free land that day. On those claims they built soddies, small houses made from blocks of mud and grass, and set up housekeeping. Germans, Irish, French, Italian, they had all emigrated to the New World in search of freedom. And they found it here in what would become Oklahoma, on the endless rolling prairie, under a big open sky.

Few of those settlers knew how difficult it would be to survive here. They didn't count on the relentless sunshine or the sweltering heat. But survive they did, and I'm here to tell you that one hundred years later, Ponca City is just about the most perfect place in all of the United States in which to grow up.

Planning for the two-day celebration had been going on for months. The weekend was to start with a Saturday morning parade through downtown, complete with bands, clowns, fire trucks, politicians in antique cars, and a real wagon train.

I'd heard nearly three hundred people—some descendants of the settlers who staked a claim in 1893, others history buffs who wanted to relive a historic moment—were already lined up on the Kansas-Oklahoma border ready to make the thirty-mile trip from Arkansas City to Ponca City: Some were walking. Some were on horseback . . . about twenty wagons in all. After the parade, city leaders would unveil a statue in front of our city hall commemorating the land run. Saturday night a picnic supper would be served on the lawn of the Marland Mansion; Sunday, a mock land run would be reenacted on the 101 Ranch Rodeo grounds.

As for me and my two best buddies—Garret Rogers, a sixteen-year-old known to drive his old Chevy as though he's competing in the Indianapolis 500, and Jimmy Joncas, a kind of slow on the uptake but very loyal fifteen-year-old—we had our own celebration planned.

Yet looking back, if I could have seen into the future that Friday afternoon, I would have climbed right back into my locker along with my overdue assignments, dirty gym socks, and that disgusting banana I should have eaten a week ago, and I would have stayed there until my spindly legs resembled frozen chicken legs crammed onto a Styrofoam plate covered in plastic wrap at the meat counter of my father's grocery store. Unfortunately, I was too far gone anticipating the prospect of an entire weekend of celebrating to take note of the nagging feeling in the pit of my stomach. I assumed I was just hungry, a normal state of being for a fifteen-year-old. Time would prove otherwise.

I slammed my locker door and fell into the flow of kids streaming out of the east door of the school. It was September, and the leaves on the trees whistled against a northerly wind rushing in from Kansas. Gusts had already released some leaves from the branches, and they could be seen dodging under and around car tires, across the bricks of Seventh Street in front of Ponca High, flitting between the bobby-socked ankles and bare legs of a giggling Rosalee and Jenna.

My two classmates were huddled together on the sidewalk, holding down their skirts with one hand and gripping their jackets closed with the other. Loose leaves blew through Rosalee's yard, fighting for their freedom against a whitewashed fence.

As I stood on the concrete steps of the school, I could see red and yellow oak leaves being whisked up into the air and forced to waltz around a chimney. The leaves joined the swirling smoke from wood burning in the fireplace at Jenna's house down the street. Finally, the leaves floated away out of sight, like fiery balloons on the crisp, cool air of fall.

The neighborhood had the look of a Norman Rockwell painting come to life, but for me the air seemed to carry a warning. This particular weekend would soon come to be etched in my mind, a notch on the proverbial belt of my life.

But at that moment, as I watched my two giggling classmates wrestle with the wind and their skirts, I couldn't see what was to come. I couldn't know that nothing would ever be the same in our small town of Ponca City, Oklahoma.

Nothing.

And no one. Especially me.

TWO

I SLIPPED MY ARMS INTO my jacket. Jenna must have sensed me staring at her, because she turned, waved, and smiled. I two-stepped it down to the sidewalk. As I approached Jenna, Rosalee took off towards her house. No surprise there. Rosalee and I had never hit it off. I think it had something to do with the time I dropped her spelling book through the sewer grate in fourth grade. It was an accident. But that's the way people are around here. They never forget anything.

"Hi Dusty," Jenna said to me, in that sweet, high-pitched voice of hers. She sounded like a little girl, but we are the same age. "My mom made some of those brownies you like."

She pushed yellow-blond strands of hair behind her ear.

"You know, with chocolate icing."

"Okay," I said.

I never could turn down food, especially her mother's brownies. We started walking toward her house, and as we crossed the street, I heard the growl of Garret's Chevy behind us. The car backfired, like a gunshot. I turned to look behind me, as the Chevy rolled up alongside us and slowed, keeping pace with Jenna and me as we walked.

"Hey Dusty!" Garret yelled over the rumble of the engine, his straw-colored mop of curls hanging out the window. "Eight o'clock at the Fun Zone?"

"No problem!" I yelled back.

He waved, gunned the engine, and left us standing in a cloud of black smoke.

We walked on down the sidewalk, not in any hurry, except I could already taste those brownies.

"Why do you hang out with that jerk?"

"I don't know," I said, with a shrug.

We'd had this conversation before, but Jenna knew me well enough by now to know that I didn't always know why I did things. And she didn't like Garret, because he hated Indians. And she, having moved here from Delaware in eighth grade, had an insatiable curiosity about Indians. I often thought that Jenna wished she were an Indian, but for what reason I couldn't say. Most of us around here don't pay any attention to them, and they kind of keep to themselves. It's just as well, I think.

With that thought, a strong gust of unseasonably cold air whipped around my legs and accelerated, nearly taking my feet out from under me. Overhead, I heard a penetrating scream. I looked up to see the most incredible white bird. It floated on the stiff wind, gliding across the sky. Its eight-foot wingspan cast a dark shadow on the street. I stopped and stared up at it. The bird circled above me, screeching, coldly staring back at me. A shiver ran down my spine and goose bumps raised on my arms.

"Look!" I said, pointing up.

Jenna glanced up. "What?"

"That huge, white bird," I said. "It looks like an eagle."

"Eagles aren't white," said Jenna, "and I don't see anything."

"Can't you hear it screaming?"

"No," she said, peering up at the sky.

6

I looked up again, and the white eagle was gone.

"You had to have heard it. Are you sure?"

"Absolutely, positively. I didn't see or hear anything."

"That's weird," I said, craning my neck, searching the sky for evidence of the white bird. I shivered again. Jenna grabbed my arm.

"Come on."

The temperature seemed to have dropped ten degrees under the shadow of the clouds. We hustled into the house, as the storm door nearly flew off its hinges. I grabbed it and followed Jenna inside.

A fire blazed in the brick fireplace in the living room. Jenna's house isn't a big house, or grand, like some of the other houses in town, but I always took off my shoes at the front door. I dropped my jacket on the arm of the couch and followed Jenna through the living room to the kitchen. Mrs. Marker was setting out glasses of cold milk at the table. I spied the plate of thick, chewy brownies on the counter. Mrs. Marker must have seen me gaping at them.

"Care for a brownie, Dusty?" she said, with a chuckle, deliberately passing them under my nose.

I sniffed the chocolaty aroma and groaned.

"I assume that means yes."

Mrs. Marker reminded me of the sitcom moms on late night cable shows. She even wore an apron over her dress. But instead of high heels, she preferred crew socks and sneakers. She smiled a big red lipstick smile and set the plate of brownies on the table.

"I've got to run out to the store, Jenna," Mrs. Marker said, removing her apron and picking up her sweater from the back of the chair. "I'll only be a few minutes."

Mrs. Marker looped her arm through the strap of her purse.

"Okay, Mom," Jenna said, in her little girl voice.

That pip-squeak of a voice made Jenna sound vulnerable, as if she was the kind of girl who needed someone to protect her, but I'd learned soon after meeting Jenna that nothing could be less true.

When I heard the front door close behind her mom, I grabbed a couple of brownies from the plate and crammed one in my mouth, followed by a long gulp of milk. I looked up to find Jenna staring at me. I'd done something wrong, but what?

"Hungry?" she asked.

"What's wrong?" I said.

"Nothing," she said, but I caught the sarcasm.

She picked up a brownie and nibbled a corner of it, making sure each crumb fell on a napkin. I stuffed the second brownie into my mouth and finished off my milk.

"What do you want to do?" I asked.

Jenna finished chewing and swallowed before answering.

"You want to play pool?"

"Okay."

I grabbed a couple more brownies in one hand. Jenna led the way down the steps to her basement and pulled the white cord that hung from the ceiling by the door. It took a moment for the fluorescent lights to come on, so I used the time to stuff another brownie into my mouth. Even with the lights on, the paneled room was dark, and what pale light there was created black shadowy silhouettes of us against the walls. I set my other brownie down on the edge of the steps and licked chocolate icing off my fingers. We each chose a pool cue, and I racked up the balls in the center of the pool table.

Jenna eyed the triangle of colored balls, leaned over, aimed her cue stick, and, with one swift motion, broke the set. Balls fell in three pockets. She stalked her next shot, like a hunter in the wilds of Africa.

"Seven-ball in the side pocket," she said.

Swish, it went in. So did the rest of them.

That's about how it went for the next hour. Occasionally, Jenna would miss a shot, and I'd get a turn to play. I never questioned why Jenna was better than me at pool. I just figured she practiced a lot, since she had her own pool table and no brothers or sisters to hog it. Jenna was the first girl who could whip the pants off me at pool. And I'm pretty good. I can beat Garret, sometimes, and he is the local champ. But then again, Garret has never played Jenna.

After we tired of playing pool, I headed home. I live on North Fifth Street, across from Pioneer Park. Growing up across from a park was great. Garret and Jimmy always wanted to come to my house because of it. We liked going to the park, especially after it rained, to play on the Big Toy's tire swing and spiral slide. It's so flat in this part of Oklahoma that after almost any rain a huge puddle forms at the bottom of the slide. We'd fly down and land with a splash in a foot-deep pool of water.

Trees fill the park, too. But the parks department workers cut off their lower branches so no one can climb them. Maybe to compensate, the city has attached long chains to the trees with swings, swings that let you soar into the sky. Sometimes when my father comes home from the grocery store, my mother will have a picnic basket ready, and we will all walk across the street and eat at one of the picnic tables in the park. We haven't done that for a long time, though. Not since the oil refinery started laying people off.

As I walked up Fifth Street towards my house, I was met by the all too familiar stink of sulphur. The oil refinery is on the south end of town, and when the wind blows north, it carries that putrid smell across Ponca City. It hasn't been as noticeable, or as frequent, since they started shutting down parts of the refinery. I guess some good has come from the cutbacks, but most of the locals either work for the refinery or own businesses that depend on the people who work for the refinery spending their money there, like my father's grocery.

Since the cutbacks, my father has steadily lost business, and he's not like he used to be. He used to take me fishing at Kaw Lake or hunting in the Ozark Mountains of Missouri. But now he works all the time. This past summer, we only took the pontoon boat out once. He laid off his assistant manager and his accountant, which had to be difficult since they had been with him since he opened the store. And now that I'm fifteen, I have to work after school and on weekends as a bag boy, bagging groceries. But not this weekend. He gave me this weekend off. I could almost taste the freedom.

I walked up the concrete driveway to our home, a large odd-shaped house with a stone wall across the front that continues on the opposite side of the driveway. That was the other reason friends always wanted to come to my house: that stone wall. It made a great fort.

The second floor of our house is covered with wood siding and painted coral. I remember pleading with my mother and father to let me camouflage it so my buddies and I could hide from the enemy better, but my parents said if we painted it jungle colors it would just stick out more, defeating the purpose. The lower level of the house is laced with sandstone. The backyard is enclosed by a wood fence, with boards placed so close together vertically that it made a perfect holding cell for our prisoners-of-war. We used the one-car garage as the general's headquarters. Like I said, a perfect setup.

I opened the side door to the house and stepped inside to the smell of chicken frying.

"Is that you, Dusty?" my mother called from the kitchen.

"Uh-huh," I said.

I threw my jacket on the rattan chest by the door and headed for the kitchen. My mother stood by the counter, patting a chicken breast into cornmeal. Her short brunette hair was curlier than usual, and she was wearing the old denim dress with pockets that she always wears when she's been cleaning.

I tugged the refrigerator door open, took a swig from the gallon jug of orange juice, put it back, and closed the door. Luckily, my mother didn't notice.

"Get washed up now and set the table," she said, with her back still to me. "Daddy will be home shortly, and he'll expect supper to be on the table. He only has an hour break."

"Yes, ma'am," I said, taking the steps two at a time to the upstairs bathroom. I picked up the comb on the sink and ran it through my short hair, wishing my hair would grow out faster. Under the sink, I found a can of mousse. After working a mound of the white foam into my hair, I ran the comb through my hair again, taking the time to look at myself from every angle, checking to see if any hairs were still askew. Satisfied I'd gotten the obstinate devils under control, I washed the remaining foam from my hands.

When I came back downstairs, the place was empty.

"Where is everybody?" I called, as I counted out five plates from the corner cabinet in the dining room and set them on the table.

"Danielle has cheerleader practice until five o'clock, and Stephanie is next door," mom answered.

She poked her head out of the kitchen.

"Be a dear and run over and get her, will you?"

"Do I have to? I'm tired," I said, frowning. I plopped into a chair.

"Is it too much to ask, after all your father and I do for you?"

Oh, jeez. Not this again. My mom gave me a look that could have frozen Mount Vesuvius in mid eruption.

"Oh, all right," I grumbled, "but remember this is supposed to be my weekend off."

I found Stephanie playing on the swing set behind Tanya's house. She and her friend were on either end of the toy, hanging from the crossbars upside down by their knees and giggling.

"It's time to come home," I said.

Stephanie's brunette curls dangled in spirals from her head, sweeping the ground as she swung back and forth. She and Tanya untangled themselves from their perches, and I started for home.

"Wait for me!" Stephanie called, running to catch up with me. "Daddy's not home yet. Why do I have to come home?"

"Mom said."

"But Daddy's not home, yet."

One thing I had learned about five-year-olds is that it doesn't pay to argue with them. They just keep repeating the same thing over and over until you think you are going to scream. So I kept repeating back, "Mom said you had to come home."

"Is Daddy home?"

"No. But Mom said to come home, now."

As our driveway came into view, Stephanie finally realized there was no turning back.

"I don't know why I have to come home now. Daddy's not even home. See? His car isn't here."

I didn't even bother answering her. We went inside, and, while Mother washed the mud from Stephanie's face and hands, I finished setting the table. I was almost done, when I heard my father's car pull in the driveway and the engine stop. When he came in, my father was smiling broader than a creek bed.

"Hey, Dusty. How's it going?" he said, striding across the room and clapping me on the back.

"Fine," I said.

Actually I was in shock. I hadn't seen my father smile like that in what seemed like forever.

"Where's your mother?" he asked.

"The bedroom," I said, smiling.

He started down the hall towards their bedroom, turned, and came back. He was still smiling but now in an apologetic way.

"I'm afraid I'm going to need your help in the store tomorrow," he said.

"But you said I could have the weekend off!"

I wasn't smiling anymore.

Neither was my dad.

"People have been calling all day, ordering roasted chickens and baked hams. If business is this good tomorrow, there won't be enough baggers to keep up."

"But I've already made plans," I said, not believing what I was hearing.

"I'm sorry, son. You'll have to change them."

"But I promised the guys I'd . . ."

"Dusty, that's the end of it."

"I don't want to hear any more about it."

He turned and walked down the hallway.

I had to get out of there.

THREE

I WALKED INTO THE FUN ZONE a few minutes before eight o'clock. The place was already packed and the noise volume was exactly the way I like it: loud. I pushed my way past the video game crowds and headed to the back of the long, narrow room. Kids from my class were playing pinball, skee-ball, and basketball—only with just the backboard and hoop. The pool tables were farther back. Garret and Jimmy had already snagged us a table and were racking up the balls.

"Hey!" I shouted, because they couldn't hear me if I didn't shout.

"You made it," Garret hollered back.

Garret had on his coolest black T-shirt and his lucky jeans, the ones with a hole in the seat. He called them his lucky jeans, because he'd almost killed himself in them once climbing a fence in the alley behind Miss Margaret Bly's house. At the time, there'd been talk that Miss Bly and Mr. Dale Rimpke, our high school principal, were engaging in . . . How shall I put this? Adult activities. Garret was trying to confirm the rumors by spying on Miss Bly, when his jeans got caught on a barb on top of the fence outside her house. That wasn't as unlucky as it sounds, because getting hung up on that barb kept him from falling into Miss Bly's yard and coming face to face with her Doberman pinscher, Spades. Miss Bly is the new town librarian, and she doesn't take kindly to kids climbing on her fence or to being spied on. For some reason, Garret refused to sit down for about a week after his encounter with the fence. Barbed wire fences can do nasty things to folk's tender parts.

I picked out a cue stick and chalked the end of it. Garret let Jimmy break the set. He knew Jimmy would be lucky to make any clean shots. Jimmy eyed the five-ball, which sat right at the edge of the corner pocket. His long brown bangs hung into his eyes. It was a touchy shot. If the cue ball hit it too hard, both balls would go in, and he would scratch, losing his turn. Jimmy blew at his bangs. His lanky frame forced him to lean way over in what appeared to me to be the most uncomfortable, contorted position I'd ever seen. It didn't, however, seem to bother him. He pulled the stick back and took his shot. He scratched.

It was my turn. Garret knew once his turn came around, the rest of us would be mostly standing and watching. I figured my angle for the six-ball and settled into position. When the cue made contact with the ball I knew it was a sinker. I made a couple more good shots, and then scratched, as the cue ball followed the ball I was aiming for into the pocket as if I had planned it that way.

I heaved a sigh and turned the table over to Garret.

Garret always drew a crowd for his turn. Kids oohed and aahed each time he sunk a ball. He rarely missed a shot, so Jimmy and I were basically reduced to spectators until he finished.

Garret was now on his last shot, the eight-ball. He had taken his time and lined up his angle clean. I could tell he felt pretty sure of himself, because he wasn't chewing on his bottom lip. If he had a tough shot to make, sometimes he'd chew his lip until it bled. He called "eight-ball in the side pocket," pulled back the stick, and was just about to pull the trigger, when someone shoved Stephen Crazy Arrow. Stephen bumped the end of Garret's pool cue, throwing off the angle. The eight-ball rolled lamely toward the side pocket and stopped. Garret had missed the call. He spun around, scarlet-faced.

"Somebody bumped my stick!"

Stephen stood alone now. Everyone else had stepped away from the table.

"Was it you, Indian boy?" Garret shouted. "You're going to pay for this!"

Garret grabbed Stephen's shirt at the neck and hoisted him into the air, shaking him hard. Stephen hung there like a side of beef on a hook. His eyes squinched together, preparing for the first blow; he was trembling down to the tips of his braids, hanging there as helpless as a baby. Nobody said one word. Then from somewhere in the thick crowd of kids, a voice shouted.

"Leave him be!"

Funny thing was I recognized that voice, though I couldn't quite put it to a face, until Jenna pushed her way through the mob. I'd never heard her speak so forcefully before.

I was shocked. And embarrassed. And scared for her.

"I said, 'Leave him be!' You big bully!"

It was clearly Jenna who'd spoken. Garret was so taken by surprise he released his grip on Stephen. Stephen fell in a quivering heap on the floor. Garret faced Jenna.

"Are you talking to me?" he said, wearing the smirk I knew so well. It was the same one he'd worn right before he'd last punched me.

"Are you hard of hearing?" she said. "Who do you think you are? Picking on Stephen like that. He didn't do it on purpose. It was an accident."

"He made me miss my shot. Now he's going to pay for it."

"How?" Jenna asked.

I had never seen her green eyes so angry.

"With Indian blood," Garret said.

"I have a better idea," Jenna said, picking up a cue stick. "You play against me. If you win, you can do what you like to Stephen. If I win, you forget the whole thing happened."

Garret laughed. A big, uproarious laugh that sent chills up my spine. When his laughter subsided, his face became serious.

"You're on."

Garret told Jimmy to rack up the balls. Jimmy jumped to it, gathering the balls into the triangle. Garret chose a different stick and chalked the end of it.

"Ladies first," Garret said.

Jenna looked over at me. I shrugged. I was not getting stuck in the middle of this one. Garret would beat the living life out of me.

Jenna broke the set and, true to form, three balls went into pockets. She set up for her next shot, calling it.

"Two-ball in the side."

It went in. She called each shot and made each shot. Each time the ball went in the pocket a cheer went up from the teens who had crowded around the table, packed together like licorice sticks. Garret seemed to shrink with each perfect sinker she made. Finally, the eight-ball was the only one remaining on the table. It sat snuggled along one long side of the table. Jenna called her shot.

"Eight-ball in the corner pocket."

The room grew quiet, as quiet as it could given the noise of the pinball machines and stereo. All eyes were on Jenna and that eight-ball. She made a pyramid with her fingers on the table, set up her angle, pulled back, and struck the cue ball. It glided easily along the table's side, tapped the eight-ball, and nudged it into motion. The eight-ball rolled the remaining length of the table and fell into the pocket. Jenna had won.

And Garret had not made one shot.

I looked across at Garret. His face was flushed with anger. He growled and stomped out of the place. Everyone cheered for Jenna. She went over to Stephen and hugged him.

I looked at Jimmy and Jimmy looked at me, and we both took

16

off after Garret. Outside I spotted Garret climbing into his car.

"Garret! Wait!"

I ran down Grand Avenue as fast as I could and grabbed onto the side of his car. He was pulling away but stopped when he saw me.

"Where you going?" I asked, gasping for breath.

"Get out of my face. You and your Indian-loving girlfriend can go to hell!"

"She's not my girlfriend," I said.

I didn't think about what I was saying at the time; I only knew I had to stop Garret from doing something stupid.

"Let's go get a burger," I said, trying to change the subject. "You've got to forget about what happened. It's a stupid game anyway. Knocking balls into pockets with a stick."

"Yeah, a stupid game," said Jimmy, who had quietly hopped into the back seat of the car. "I'm starving, man."

Garret's expression softened.

"Is that all you think about? Your stomach?"

He threw a look over his shoulder at Jimmy. Jimmy sat there rubbing his belly.

"Okay, but it's got to be greasy or nothing," Garret said. "Hop in, Dusty."

I hopped in the car, and he hit the gas. The wheels of the car squealed as we pulled away from the curb. Jenna was coming out of the Fun Zone with her arm hooked through Stephen's, as we drove away. I know she saw me, because Garret's car backfired right in front of them. She looked up, but I couldn't read her expression. I also couldn't keep from staring at her. It was beyond my understanding how she could want to touch that Indian, much less be seen hanging on him like that in public.

Garret must not have seen Jenna and Stephen, because he didn't say anything more. Instead, he drove down Grand Avenue, cruising through town. It was nearing ten o'clock, and the cruising traffic had begun to thicken. He turned north on Fifth Street and followed

17

it to Hartford Avenue. The drive-in was on the corner. He pulled into an empty space and pushed the intercom. He ordered burgers, onion rings, and sodas. While we waited for the waitress to bring our food, we listened to music on the stereo. Garret's speakers are great. Sometimes when we cruise through town, he'll turn his bass up so loud it is like being in the middle of an earthquake.

Garret turned to me.

"I don't know why you hang around with that Jenna girl."

"I don't know, either," I said.

The last thing I wanted to talk about was Jenna.

FOUR

I HAD DIFFICULTY DRAGGING myself out of bed at five o'clock the next morning, especially since I'd spent most of the night lost in some horrible nightmare. Twice I had woken in a cold sweat. All I could remember was being on a wagon train surrounded by howling Indians. It must have been that greasy burger and onion rings I'd eaten at the drive-in. Then I remembered about Jenna and Stephen.

I showered and dressed quickly, grabbed an apple muffin from the basket on the kitchen counter and quietly closed the back door behind me.

It was still dark outside and the street lights were on. I wheeled my bicycle out of the garage and hopped on the seat, fitting my feet to the pedals as I drifted down the driveway and onto the sidewalk on Fifth Street. I rode south on Fifth, holding the handlebar with one hand and the muffin with the other. Finishing my breakfast in three bites, I wiped my hand on my jeans and grabbed the handlebars tightly with both hands, pedaling hard to climb the slight incline between Hazel Avenue and Broadway. When I reached the intersection, I looked both ways and popped a wheelie off the curb and onto the street. Not a soul was in sight; no cars, no people, only me. Morning is my favorite time of day. It's so quiet and still. The cool, damp air tickled my skin as I breezed along, coasting to Cleveland Avenue. Another block to Grand Avenue. I could smell sausage cooking at Grand Café. I looked in the window as I passed by, and Mr. Coates waved back at me from his usual spot at the grill. I stopped at Grand and peered to my right.

Between Second and Third streets a grandstand to hold the city dignitaries had been set up for the weekend's parade. The centennial parade would come straight up Grand Avenue—from First Street all the way to Fifth. I wondered if I'd get to see any of it, or if I'd be stuck in the grocery store all day and miss it. Garret and Jimmy would be sore at me, but like my father says business is business.

I heard the 5:30 a.m. train whistle blow. I've been told you can hear that whistle from every corner of the city. The Santa Fe runs right through Ponca City between First Street and Union Avenue. I set my watch by its comings and goings.

It's about sixteen blocks to the store from my house. I was only halfway there. My dad would be waiting for me to arrive, so he could concentrate on getting the store open. I crossed Grand and pumped the pedals hard, trying to make up time. My calf-muscles burned. I knew dad would be busy in the stockroom. With Roy gone, he had to meet the Saturday delivery truck at 4:30 a.m. every week.

The neon sign that read "Hamilton Grocers" was still on when I pulled into the store's parking lot—empty, except for my father's Buick. I pedaled my bike around to the back of the store and found my dad unloading boxes from a semi-trailer.

"The delivery truck was late this morning," he said. "I need you to unload the rest of this, so I can get the store opened."

I hopped up on the long trailer bed and began unloading cartons of cereal boxes, vegetables, dairy products, paper towels; you name it, I carried it into the stock room. Once it was all unloaded,

I marked off each item on the inventory sheet. Then I loaded it all on a dolly and carted the goods to their specified aisle in the store.

Tom, the stockman, took care of stocking the shelves, but he didn't come to work until 6:30 a.m. on Saturday. I was glad I didn't have to do that, as well. My father was up front counting the money in each of the three cash register drawers. He likes to double check them every day. As I watched him, I realized I was almost as tall as him now though not as broad across the shoulders.

Dad went from one checkout line to the next, bent in concentration, now and then shoving the silver frames of his eyeglasses up on the bridge of his nose. His dark hair was slicked into place and glistened under the bright lights. His hands worked rapidly with the cash, shuffling the ones, fives, and tens from one hand to the other. He could have been attaching a lure to the end of his fishing line, so comfortable he seemed. I wish he were. I wish I was. The store opens at 7 a.m. on weekends, 6 a.m. during the week, and my father is here every morning. No chance we'd be going fishing anytime soon.

At a quarter to seven, the cashiers began arriving. Mrs. Gary, a grandmother, has a ton of children who have all grown up and moved away from Ponca City. She likes to show me pictures of them and their children every chance she gets. I know she misses them a lot. Penny, a mom-to-be, is due to deliver her baby in a few months. She's been pretty grumpy lately; although, if I had to carry around a basketball in my stomach all the time I guess I'd be grumpy, too. Janelle, a senior at Ponca High, works after school and on Saturdays. Her mother won't let her work on Sundays, because she has to go to church.

At seven o'clock my father unlocked the front door of the store, and a line of people filed in. My father smiled, greeting each one by name. He knows everyone in Ponca City.

I was nearly finished with my tasks, when I was paged over the loudspeaker. I ran up to the front of the store. Mrs. Gray's checkout line was backed up to the middle of aisle three. She needed help bagging groceries. I started stuffing items into paper sacks and carrying them out to the customers' cars. My favorite part of bagging groceries is tips. Not everyone tips the sackers, because helping the customers with their groceries to their cars is part of our job and a service the store offers. But, occasionally, a customer will not take no for an answer.

With my work under control, my mind began to chew on odd snippets of what had happened yesterday at the Fun Zone and after school. I kept thinking about Jenna asking me why I hang out with Garret. It wasn't an easy question to answer, if only because he and I have known each other most of our lives.

We've always been friends, since first grade. He was held back from second grade, and so we ended up in the first grade together, despite him being a year older than me. I was kind of scrawny back then, and the other kids in my class picked on me. Garret was big for his age and older than the rest of our fellow first-graders, but he had trouble with reading. I guess that's why he was held back. The teacher asked me to help him. I did. We became friends. And no one ever picked on me again.

By ten o'clock, my arms were aching from all the lifting and sorting and carrying. I noticed a lull in business and headed to the window ledge at the front of the store to rest for a spell. Tom, who had also been bagging groceries, came over to me.

"Your dad wants to see you," he said, pointing at the office.

I heard someone whistling and turned to look. It was my father. He was waving his arms at me. I walked over to a space about five-feet square on a raised platform that enabled my dad to overlook the entire store. He unlocked the door from inside. I stepped up into his office.

"I need you to help those customers," he said.

He nodded toward a Ponca family trailing down aisle four.

"Make sure they go through the checkout line, if you know what I mean. And watch their hands. They have a tendency to put them in their pockets a lot."

He opened the office door, and I stepped down. I made my way through the customers and carts to aisle four. Four Indians rounded the shelves and turned right. I tried not to be too conspicuous watching them. I always felt weird doing it, but father knows best. The weathered-skinned matriarch wore a single braid that hung down to the hem of her blouse. A younger woman, probably about my mother's age, held the elder's elbow.

I recognized the guy and girl with them as Cindy and Leslie. They both went to Ponca High. Cries For War was their last name. I remembered because kids tease them about it. Inside their cart were only a few items: a bag of rice, potatoes, dried corn, and a sack of chips.

The old woman could barely walk even with the help of her daughter, but the guy and girl still lingered behind her, making slow progress through the canned fruit section. I felt ridiculous following them, pretending to straighten items on the shelves while actually watching their hands, as instructed. When Cindy and Leslie each threw a scowl in my direction, I was so ashamed I wanted to hide— or project myself onto one of those spaghetti sauce labels featuring an Italian mama serving pasta to her family.

Finally, the family inched toward the checkout line. I let out a sigh of relief. My mortifying task completed, I walked over to the office and knocked on the door.

"I don't know what I would have done without you today, son," my father said, when he saw me. "It's beginning to slow down. So, if you want to take off, it's okay with me."

He patted my shoulder.

"You worked hard today."

"Thanks, Dad." I didn't give him time to change his mind.

The store had been busy all day with people doing last minute shopping for the picnic supper and other anniversary gatherings, and if I hung around too long it might get busy again. I quickly untied my red apron and hung it up for next time.

"Can I take some candy bars for the guys?" I asked.

23

"Sure," my dad said. "Have fun at the parade!"

I grabbed a fistful of candy bars, stuffed them in a paper sack, and headed for the stockroom where I had stashed my bicycle. I tucked my T-shirt in the waistband of my jeans and stowed the bag of candy down the front of it. I wheeled my bicycle outside, hopped on, and then pedaled hard down Oklahoma Avenue to Fifth Street. I hit every green light—yep, my luck was changing. I could feel it.

I coasted past the fire station looking for Garret and Jimmy. Jimmy's dad is a fireman, and sometimes the guys were known to hang out with the firemen sitting in lawn chairs in front of the firehouse, waiting for a call. But not today. I didn't see them anyplace.

When I reached Grand Avenue, the main street through town and today's parade route, barricades had been set up across Fifth Street. Spectators waiting for the parade packed the sidewalks along Grand. The parade was supposed to begin at ten o'clock, starting on First Street and ending at Fifth.

I looked down Grand Avenue to my left, searching for any sign of the parade, but apparently it had yet to start. I looked next to my right at the plaza where the statue was to be unveiled and did a double take. What appeared to be every member of the local Ponca tribe sat cross-legged on the ground in a circle around the tarp-draped statue. Nearby Ponca City policemen barked into their walkie-talkies and paced back and forth.

I nearly fell off my bicycle when Jenna waved at me from the circle of protestors. She was sitting with them next to Stephen Crazy Arrow. The only non-Indian in the group, she stuck out, like a patch of cotton in a wheat field.

She motioned for me to come over, but I shook my head. She must have seen the fear that flashed across my face, because she stood up and jogged towards me wearing a big smile. "Scared to come and sit with the Indians? They don't scalp people anymore," she said.

"I know that. I'm supposed to meet someone here, and I didn't want them to see . . . ahh miss me."

24

"You mean you didn't want Garret and Jimmy to see you sitting with the Poncas," she said.

"What's going on over there?" I asked, changing the subject.

"It's a sit-in. The Ponca are protesting about the statue."

"What's wrong with it?"

"Nothing's wrong with the statue," Jenna said. "It's the inscription they don't like."

"What does it say?"

"It says, 'This land is mine.' "

"What's wrong with that?"

"In the words of Chief Seattle, 'How can you buy the sky? How can you own the rain and the wind?' "

"I don't understand."

"The earth does not belong to us. We belong to the earth."

"But this land was claimed by the settlers. That's what the whole celebration is about," I said.

"Yes, and we herded Native Americans, like the Ponca, onto reservations in order to claim the land." She tilted her head in the direction of her fellow protestors. "That's what they're upset about."

"We can't give it back now," I said.

"They don't want it back. They just don't want the statue to say, 'This land is mine.' "

"What difference does it make after a hundred years?"

"It's a matter of respect. Respect for their beliefs. We have a different understanding of them now than we did in 1893."

"What is past is past. We can't be held responsible for what our ancestors did." I heard myself mouthing my father's words.

"No. We had no control over that. But we are responsible for our own actions. Perhaps, in some small way, fixing the inscription would show that we're sorry they were forced to make so many sacrifices."

Jenna rocked back and forth on the balls of her feet.

"Don't look now, but I think your good buddies just ducked behind that brick wall across the street."

I spun around to look, and, before I could remind Jenna that I'd meet her at the picnic that evening, she was already jogging back to join the circle of people around the statue.

I pedaled across Fifth Street to the brick wall in front of the Chamber of Commerce building and spotted Garret and Jimmy trotting down the alley behind the row of buildings that fronted Grand Avenue. I pedaled hard and caught up to them.

"Where you going?" I asked.

"The wagon train is coming," Garret said, "and I have a surprise for the drivers."

"What kind of surprise?" I asked.

Jimmy laughed.

"A big surprise!"

Garret and Jimmy were running hard now, but I kept pace with them on my bicycle. We crossed Fourth Street. No sign of the wagon train. We heard the Ponca High School Band playing a few blocks away. We reached Third Street and saw the drum major lifting his baton high in the air, above the crowd lining Grand Avenue, keeping the beat of the music.

Garret waved his hand at us, signaling for us to keep going. At Second Street we turned right and headed towards Grand Avenue. Garret was acting weird, hiding behind trees and in doorways, inching his way to Grand. The crowd blocked the street and sidewalks. Garret wound his way through the mass of humanity. Jimmy stuck to him, like pine sap. I had to get off my bicycle and push it through the crowd. By the time I caught up to them, Garret had wormed his way to a front row spot.

The first wagon—of some twenty or more covered wagons in the wagon train—was only fifty feet away from us, rolling slowly up Grand Avenue to waves of cheers from the spectators.

The metal wheels of the wagon ground against the pavement, and its axles creaked and groaned. A team of four matching bay horses strained against the leather harnesses, drawing the first wagon ever closer to us. The clip clop of hooves hitting the street echoed against the tall brick storefronts, like hail on a tin roof. The horses held their heads high, their strong thick necks arched majestically. Their ears stood at attention, but their necks swung from side to side, as if to better see the gaping-mouthed children who lined the streets.

The day was warm, and sweat glistened on the withers of the horses. Their long coarse, black tails whipped back and forth—efficiently dispensing the flies swarming at their haunches.

The wagon master, covered in dust but shaded under the wide brim of his Stetson, sat with his back straight, high on a plank seat, a long, braided leather whip in one hand and reins held loosely in the other. Beside him, another cowboy guarded a sack of candy at his feet from which he extracted handfuls of treats to toss into the crowd. Horses and riders of all ages trailed along beside and behind the wagon as far as the eye could see. It was going to be awhile before the three hundred visitors, who had made the two-day ride from Arkansas City, passed through town.

Garret waited until the wagon train drew closer. He looked both ways and slid his hand into his jacket pocket. When he pulled his hand out of his pocket, it held a fistful of round black firecrackers. He handed some to Jimmy and some to me, and then before I could say anything, he raised his hand over his head and slammed one, two, three, four of them onto the pavement in front of the first team of horses.

The fireworks went off with a bang, each one in succession, like tiny bombs, spraying sparks in the air as they exploded. Jimmy, for all his deficiencies in the brain department, was endowed with the best pitching arm in Ponca City and, with perfect aim, delivered his firecrackers, like two fast balls, directly between the forefeet of the two lead horses. It was the first time I'd ever seen a horse leave the ground so far behind, and I saw not one but two of them leap four feet off the pavement and into the air.

The lead horses were harnessed together on either side of a wooden beam and connected to the pair of horses behind them.

When the lead horses leapt, the rear pair had to leap, as well. The end result was not good. The covered wagon began swaying back and forth—taking the wagon master so by surprise that he lost his grip on the reins. The reins fell out of his reach and onto the ground, landing between the hooves of the horses.

The crowd began screaming and running. As for the two lead horses, well, when they finally returned to earth they were a good ten feet in front of the spot where the firecrackers had sent them airborne, and they hit the ground at a gallop.

The Ponca High School Band continued to play a rousing Sousa march and—being unable to hear the commotion behind them—stayed in step, blocking the course of the runaway covered wagon. Meanwhile, the horses, no longer constrained by a driver, took a detour around the band and careened into the grandstand of dignitaries.

It was too much for the grandstand. Its rear supports crumpled, and it toppled backwards, dumping the mayor and other very important people screaming onto the sidewalk.

The covered wagon, not being very steady to begin with, eventually fell on its side, slowing the horses' progress. Not that they didn't try. The horses dragged the wagon on its side for quite a ways until finally coming to a stop, then rearing up wild-eyed and disoriented.

Children cried, dogs barked, police whistles blew. People scattered to the four winds. I was in such a state of shock that I stood there for a split second with my mouth agape, while Garret and Jimmy took off in the opposite direction. Not knowing what else to do, I ran after them, as though I were guilty by association.

We didn't stop running until we reached an old abandoned Santa Fe railroad boxcar hidden behind a mountainous pile of metal scraps between Union Avenue and the railroad tracks. We scrambled inside and fell on the straw-covered floor.

Garret, Jimmy, and I took one look at each other and burst out laughing, gasping for breath and holding our aching sides. The boxcar smelled of livestock, and it was so hot I thought I was going to melt. We would settle down enough to breathe evenly, only to have Jimmy say something like, "Did you see the look on the mayor's face?" He would widen his eyes to the size of shooter marbles, and twist and contort his mouth as though he were silently screaming, and we would bust our sides with laughter again. We might have continued like that for longer had not a churning in the pit of my stomach suddenly taken the laugh right out of me.

"Hey, I almost forgot about these," I said. I reached in my shirt and pulled out the bag of candy bars. I opened the sack and groaned in disappointment. "They're melted."

"So what," Garret said.

He grabbed the bag away from me, dug his hand down into the gooey chocolate, and brought out a handful of rich, dark sweet slime. He licked the chocolate off and passed the bag to Jimmy.

"Hey, Dusty," Jimmy said, eating chocolate off the palm of his hand. "Where's your bike?"

"Oh no!" I said. "I left it at the parade."

"I bet one of them Indians done stole it already," Garret said.

He reached into his pocket and pulled out a switchblade. At the touch of his finger, the blade sprung open. Its tip had a slight curve.

"Where did you get that?" I asked.

"I've been carrying it around ever since the Indians started circling over that statue deal," Garret said. "You like it?"

He rotated the blade in his hand.

"It's neat," I said.

"You better close it up before somebody gets hurt," Jimmy said.

"You afraid of a little knife?" Garret asked, angling it closer to Jimmy's face.

"Course not." Jimmy lowered his eyes and dug his hand into the bag of chocolate, again.

"Maybe my bike is still there," I said, standing up. "We have to find it."

I tugged open the boxcar door and poked out my head to see if we were still alone or if company had arrived.

"I don't hear any more whistles or anything," I said. "Maybe everyone went home."

"Are you nuts?" Garret said. "You go back there now and, sure as I'm sitting here, the police are going to grab you by the shirt collar and haul your behind to jail."

He closed the blade of the knife and shoved it back into the pocket of his jeans.

"No way," I said, but I had that sinking feeling again in the pit of my stomach. Garret was probably right; he knew a lot more about these things than I did.

"My dad's going to use me for fish bait," I said.

"Tell him some Indian stole it, while you were watching the commotion at the parade," Garret said.

"He would believe that," I said, "but I need that bike to get to the store."

"I'll go back with you," Jimmy said, dropping the now empty candy bag on the floor.

"You're both crazy as a marmot," Garret said. "You think you can just stroll up the street and nobody will notice you?"

"Everyone was watching the parade. They weren't paying us no mind," Jimmy said.

Sometimes Jimmy could surprise me with his figuring.

"That's right," I said. "I bet nobody even noticed us. I've got to try. You guys coming?"

Jimmy stood up. Garret frowned at him, and I thought for a minute Jimmy was going to change his mind.

"Yeah, I'm with you," Jimmy said.

"Well, I'm not," Garret said. "I have more important things to do than chase after baby's old bike. Do you still suck your thumb, too?"

"Only when nobody's watching," I said, giving it right back to him.

Sometimes Garret could get in a mood, but I didn't let it bother me. Jimmy and I hopped out of the boxcar. No one was around, so we headed back toward Grand Avenue as though nothing had happened.

"Do you think Garret's scared?" Jimmy asked, kicking a crumpled tin can with his toe.

"No. He's probably got to fiddle with his car," I said.

But deep down, I thought Jimmy was closer to the truth than either of us wanted to admit.

FIVE

JIMMY AND I WANDERED up and down Grand Avenue, peering down alleys and peeking around corners—all in hopes of finding my bicycle. Most of the parade spectators were long gone, and the street had almost resumed its normal Saturday traffic flow. Only the right lane was still blocked by a crew dismantling what was left of the grandstand and loading the remains of it onto a flatbed truck. We were too afraid to ask if anyone had seen my bicycle for fear someone might connect us to the firecrackers.

"I bet someone turned it into the police station," Jimmy said. "I lost my bike once, and that's where it was."

"Yes, but if we go there it would be like putting our heads in a noose," I said.

"What are you going to do?" Jimmy asked.

"I don't know," I said. "I just don't know."

"I'm sorry we couldn't find your bike, Dusty."

"Thanks for coming with me."

"It was nothing," said Jimmy.

We stood there on the corner of Second Street and Grand, not knowing what to say after that.

"I best be getting home," Jimmy said.

"Me, too."

"Are you going to the picnic supper?" Jimmy asked.

I nodded. "I promised Jenna I'd go with her."

"Oh."

Jimmy lived on the south end of town, so he turned around and began walking down Second Street. He had only gone a few steps when he stopped and turned to face me.

"Maybe I'll see you there."

"Okay."

I waved good-bye and walked north on Second Street until I reached Hazel Avenue. I followed it three blocks to Fifth Street. As I neared my house, my stomach grumbled and not only because I was hungry. How was I going to explain what had happened to my bike?

I reached my driveway and saw my father's car wasn't in the garage. A wave of relief washed over me and my steps became lighter. I opened the back door and looked around. I could hear my mother in the kitchen. Good aromas filled my nostrils, and I breathed them in.

"Is that you, Dusty?" my mother called.

I heard pots and pans rattling around. "Yes, ma'am."

Stephanie came skipping out of the kitchen, a broad smile on her face. "Dusty! Dusty! You're home!" She wrapped her arms around my legs and squeezed me tightly. "We're getting our picnic ready. I'm helping."

"Oh, thank heavens you're all right." My mother peeked around the corner of the kitchen, drying her hands on a dish towel. "What happened to your shirt?"

I glanced down at my shirt front and realized some of the chocolate had leaked out of the bag of candy bars and onto it. My shirt was also covered with bits of straw and dirt from the boxcar.

"I tripped on the way home," I said.

"How many times?" Danielle asked, as she came bounding down the staircase.

"Ha ha, very funny. You're a regular comedian."

She did look a little like a clown in her florescent pink miniskirt and eye-popping yellow T-shirt, a shirt nearly as long as the skirt she wore. As usual, she had a hairbrush in her hand.

"About time you got home," she said. "Did you hear what happened at the parade?"

I shook my head, afraid to speak. Danielle bent over, letting gravity work on her long auburn hair, before brushing it into a ponytail.

"Some idiot set off firecrackers in front of the wagon train," Danielle said. She stood up, holding her hair in one hand and wrapping it in an elastic band with the other.

"I thought we were going to be trampled!" She wrinkled her nose and sniffed. "What's that smell?"

"You?" I said, brokenly.

"It's not me!" she said. "I just took a shower. It must be you."

"I meant *you* were in the parade?"

"I don't know why I'm surprised that you forgot I was going to be in the parade."

I gave her my usual shrug of apology.

"I swear, Dusty. You'd forget to breathe if it weren't an automatic reflex."

"I had to work this morning," I said. "Was anyone hurt?"

"No. Thank goodness," she said. "It was a miracle that the people on the grandstand weren't hurt though. The whole thing collapsed when the horses tried to go underneath and over it. The mayor was beside herself! Whoever did it is in big trouble when they catch him. If it hadn't been so dangerous, it might have been comical. You smell like a barn."

"If you plan to go to the picnic, you'd better get cleaned up," my mother said from the kitchen.

"Yeah, you'll kill everyone's appetite if you go smelling like that," Danielle chimed in. She pinched her nose with her fingers and ran back up the stairs.

"And you'll blind everyone with that outfit!" I yelled after her.

"Oh, be quiet," she yelled back.

I heard her bedroom door slam, then moseyed into the kitchen and opened the refrigerator door.

"Got anything to eat? I'm starved."

"Not before you clean up. What in the world were you doing?" My mother asked, as she packed food into plastic containers and loaded them into the ice chest on the floor. On the floor, Stephanie stacked the containers inside, like a tower of wooden blocks.

"But I'm starving," I said.

"Have a banana," my mother said, "and be sure to bring those clothes down to the laundry room when you finish your shower. They'll smell up the whole house if I don't wash them right away."

"When is dad getting home?" I asked.

"He's going to meet us at the Marland Mansion."

"Good."

I grabbed a banana and peeled it on my way up the steps. It would be dark by the time my father got home after the picnic supper. He probably wouldn't realize my bicycle was missing until tomorrow morning, and maybe by then, I could come up with a good excuse—or, even better, I'd have found it.

Despite what my sister said, I hadn't noticed any unnatural odor until I started taking off my shirt. A good whiff confirmed she had been being kind. I stank. Worse than the condition of my clothes, however, was that I had forgotten about Danielle being in the parade. As much as she gets on my nerves, I wouldn't want anything bad to happen to her.

And that is exactly what could have happened.

I undressed and peeked out my bedroom door. Danielle's door was closed, and for once the bathroom door was open. I tiptoed into the hallway in my underwear, but before I could reach the bathroom and close the door, I heard a catcall coming from downstairs. I turned to look.

Stephanie was smiling up at me.

"I see you!" She giggled.

I rushed inside the bathroom, stubbing my little toe on the door as I slammed it closed. I hollered in pain. If I hadn't been in such agony, I would have chuckled.

I showered, dressed, and went downstairs in time to help load the picnic basket and ice chest into the back of the van. Stephanie had an armload of what she calls her "little sisters." The girl owns more dolls than any girl I know, and they are usually lined up somewhere in different stages of healing. One may be wrapped from head to foot in toilet tissue, recovering from some horrible accident, while another will have bandages covering imaginary scrapes on various appendages. Stephanie has quite an imagination when it comes to injuries.

Danielle had already left with her latest boyfriend, Jack, if I remembered his name correctly. I can't keep track of who is her current beau and who is last week's news. Jack competes in rodeos as a calf roper; he would be in the mock land run at the 101 Ranch Rodeo grounds tomorrow . . . on Sunday. I had to keep reminding myself what day it was. So much had happened, and it was only Saturday. I had been looking forward to this weekend for weeks, the whole weekend free to do what I wanted. But it was quickly turning out to be the worst weekend of my life.

We arrived at the Marland Mansion and a parking lot packed with cars. Streams of people carried picnic baskets, blankets, folding chairs, and ice chests around to the back of the mansion where the picnic was to take place. I made two trips back to the car before everything was on our blanket. Mom had chosen a spot under an old oak tree. Stephanie had spread out a baby blanket and lined up her "little sisters" for their picnic.

Mr. and Mrs. Marker and Jenna—their arms laden with their own provisions—approached us, and I ran to help them. Jenna was carrying a wicker picnic basket, a blanket, and two folding chairs. I grabbed the basket and the folding chairs from her, and we walked back to where our blanket was spread out on the ground.

"Hi, Mrs. Hamilton," Jenna said.

"Hi, Jenna," said my mother, giving her a hug. "Here, let me help you spread out that blanket."

Mr. and Mrs. Marker came up and set their chairs and ice chest down near ours. Mrs. Marker hugged my mother and looked around.

"Beautiful evening for a picnic," she said. "After that cold front blew through here yesterday, I was worried I'd have to dig sweaters out of storage for us to wear tonight."

"That was strange," my mother said. "It certainly didn't stay around long, though. I think it hit ninety degrees at eight o'clock this morning. I'm so glad it cooled down a bit. I was afraid it was going to be miserable sitting outside tonight, especially here along the creek, with the mosquitoes so thick this year."

Mr. Marker nodded and began setting up the lawn chairs on the grass. "Were you at the parade earlier?" he asked.

"Yes," my mother said. "Danielle was in front of the band with the other cheerleaders when it happened. Scared me to death. I thought surely she was going to be run over, if not by the horses and wagons, then by the people trying to get out of the way."

Jenna looked at me as though she knew what had happened, but for the life of me, I didn't know how she could know. I brushed the thought off as impossible; I was being paranoid.

"Why don't we go over to where the band is setting up," Jenna said to me.

"Okay."

"Don't be long you two. Dusty, your father will be here any minute, and we'll be ready to eat," my mother said.

"Okay," I said.

Jenna and I ambled down the slight incline toward the wooden band stand. The sun shone in our eyes, as it made its way westward; it would soon drop behind the roof of the Marland Mansion. I shaded my eyes with my hand as we approached the platform. Haley and The Prairie Dons were to play during and after the picnic, and I expected a lot of people would be kicking up their heels to the country music before the night was over. Me, I was never much for dancing.

"You know," Jenna said, looking at me out of the corner of her eye, "they decided to postpone the unveiling of the statue until next week."

"They did? Why?"

"After the parade fiasco, I guess they figured they better quit while they were ahead. They think some Indian kids threw the firecrackers at the wagon train."

We watched members of the band set up their speakers and connect their microphones to them.

"How do they know that?" I asked. "Did anyone see who did it?"

"I don't know. But this deal with the statue has everyone stirred up, both Indian and white."

"It could have been anybody, then."

"Exactly," Jenna said.

The four men crawling all over the stage were dressed identically in fancy, black western shirts studded with rhinestones and trimmed with gold fringe; they all wore black jeans and high-priced boots. Black Stetsons perched on their heads. Standing a little apart was their female singer, Haley. What a vision.

She wore a poofy skirt similar to the one my Aunt Betty wears for square dancing, and her red hair hung to the middle of her back, like a waterfall. Her shirt was the same as the men's, but it puffed out in all the right places; I almost hypnotized myself watching the gold fringe of her outfit sway back and forth. Slender calves rose out of gold cowboy boots, leading the eye to her slim thighs. Her waist was the size of Stephanie's. She was the most beautiful woman I had ever seen.

Jenna caught me staring at the singer and punched me in the ribs

39

with her elbow—hard enough to take my breath away.

"Your ogling is impolite," she said. "What you need is a cowboy hat to shade your eyes. Then you could stare as much as you like and no one would be able to tell."

"So that's why everyone around here wears those broad-brims," I said.

Jenna laughed. "I thought everybody knew that."

Someone tugged on my jeans and I looked down. It was my little sister. "We're ready to eat," she announced.

Stephanie took my hand and Jenna's and led us back to the blanket, where dinner was being served. The big lawn was now a patchwork of families on colorful blankets, spreads, and quilts stretching to the edge of the nearby woods and creek.

My father sat beside my mother in a lawn chair.

"Hi, Dad," I said, as casually as I could. He glared at me from under thick dark brows; his eyeglasses had slipped down on his nose once again.

"I hear there was some excitement at the parade today," he said.

"That's what they say."

"Were you able to see what happened?" he asked, raising his eyebrows.

"Not really."

"I hope they catch the scoundrel responsible for spoiling the parade. After all the work those volunteers put into planning it, it's sinful behavior. People could have been hurt."

I nodded.

"Lots of food here," my mother said, handing me a plate.

I found an open spot on the blanket, sat down, and began piling cold ham, deviled eggs, potato salad, coleslaw, pickled beets, and homemade rolls onto my plate. My attention then turned to devouring every last morsel.

I was considering seconds, when the band let loose with a rip-roaring song that demanded attention. Jenna and I decided to mosey on down a bit closer to the stage. People were singing along, and a few couples were dancing on the grass in front of the stage. Haley was busy winning hearts. I swear every male eye in the place was locked on her. Her wail carried a twang that would have made Pasty Cline proud, and, though I knew better, as we neared the stage, I could swear she was singing just to me.

The sky was now a purple-red twilight. Stars began appearing overhead and a full moon illuminated the place. As luck would have it, Jimmy showed up just as Haley reached the crooning part of her song.

"Hey, Dusty!" Jimmy said.

He acknowledged Jenna with a nod. She nodded back at him, then averted her eyes and appeared to concentrate on the band.

"You need a lift home?" he asked me.

I frowned at Jimmy and tilted my head in Jenna's direction.

"No, not really," I said.

Jenna was still staring at the band. Jimmy took the hint and said in a quieter voice, "Garret thought you might like to practice driving."

My ears perked up.

"He's going to let me drive his Chevy?"

"That's what he said. You interested?"

"I don't know."

My eyes were glued once again to Haley's fringe, and I was reluctant to pull them away.

"You see that lady singer up there?" I asked Jimmy.

"Yeah, she's hot."

"I was kind of enjoying the view, if you know what I mean."

"Make up your mind quick-like," Jimmy said. "Garret doesn't make these offers too often. I'd hate to see you miss a chance like this."

"It's mighty tempting, but . . ."

"You're not still sore about your bike, are you?" Jimmy asked.

I could have slugged him right then and there. What if Jenna had heard him? I glanced over at her, but she was still swaying to the

41

music, absorbed by the performance. I took Jimmy by the arm and pulled him a few yards away from Jenna, out of earshot.

"All I need is for Jenna to overhear you talking about . . . that."

Jenna was big sister and mother all rolled into one, and her wrath would be the wrath of two people, too.

"Are you coming or not?" Jimmy said.

I gazed at Haley trying to decide what I should do. I hated to turn down a chance to drive that turbo-boosted Chevy. Garret had installed dual cams a few months before, and, with just a light touch on the gas pedal, he could lay tracks on the road for fifty feet. Still, the Haleys of the world don't come my way very often. But realistically what chance did I have with a girl like her? Driving Garret's car, however, had been a dream of mine forever.

"I'm in," I said. "Where is he?"

"He's parked along Monument, by the iron gates."

"Okay. Give me a few minutes, and I'll meet you there."

"Great."

Jimmy took off into the crowd, and I turned my attention to my new problem. I needed a quick getaway excuse, one Jenna would buy. As luck would have it, when I reached her, Rosalee was there, too, swaying to the music alongside Jenna.

"Hi, Rosalee," I said.

I didn't even have to force a smile, because Rosalee had provided me with an out. Jenna's eyes narrowed when she saw me smiling broadly, so I toned it down. I didn't want to appear too happy to see Rosalee, or Jenna would know something was up. I swear that girl has a sixth sense when it comes to tomfoolery.

"Isn't it a great band?" I said to the girls.

"What would you know about it?" Rosalee said.

I resisted the inclination to respond with my normal sarcasm; instead I grinned pleasantly.

"I thought you'd be out there dancing by now."

"I've been trying to talk Jenna into helping me get a line dance started, but . . ."

"That's a wonderful idea!" I said. "Jenna, you love line dancing. Go ahead. Why don't you join Rosalee?"

"What about you?" she asked.

"Me? I'm not into dancing. I always end up tripping someone or stepping on someone's toes. You go ahead and don't worry about me. I'll be fine."

Rosalee's face registered surprise, as if she couldn't believe her good luck. Dusty, her arch enemy, was supporting her efforts to cajole Jenna to dance. Before anyone could question my motives, I waved bye-bye to Jenna with my index finger, as Rosalee pulled her by the arm towards the grassy dance floor. Jenna's ears turned red with anger. She glanced back at me once; I blew her a kiss. She shook her fist at me and gave me the most hateful look.

I edged my way out of the crowd now ringing the impromptu dance floor and walked around the mansion toward the front parking lot. I quickened my steps up the short incline and across the wide expanse of pavement. When I reached the iron gates that opened onto Monument, I heard the rumble of the Chevy. I ran the few remaining steps to the car and leaned in the passenger-side window.

"Police!" I yelled.

Jimmy jumped, as I expected he would, then snorted when he realized it was only me, as I also knew he would. He began hiccuping after every other breath, and Garret and I roared with laughter each time.

"Hop in," Garret said.

I opened the rear passenger door, slid in, and slammed the door shut. Garret gunned the engine, pulling away from the curb so fast the car left black streaks on the pavement as we drove away.

I don't know what it is about the roar of a finely tuned engine, the squeal of tires against pavement, and the feel of the cool evening air hitting my face that heightens the senses, but even now I wouldn't trade those untroubled, heedless minutes for an ocean of wisdom.

For as I look back now, I realize they were the last poignant moments of my adolescence, the beginning of the end of what I now refer to—thanks to my French class—as the *Rencontrer* era of my life. You see *rencontrer* means a contest between forces. And, in my case, the forces at work on my life were still unknown at the time Garret, Jimmy, and I decided to go joyriding.

They wouldn't become clear to me until after my next encounter with the white eagle.

Six

ARE YOU SURE YOU WANT me to drive?" I asked, when Garret slid into the front passenger seat of the Chevy. I was sitting behind the steering wheel. The radio was playing one of my favorite tunes; it put me in a good mood, giddy with feelings I'd never known before. I wrapped my fingers around the steering wheel, repeatedly tightening and releasing my grip. We were parked along the curb at the corner of South Ash and Otoe Avenue, directly under a street light.

Garret punched a knob on the dashboard, and the stereo went dead.

"Do you want to learn how to drive or not?" Garret said.

"Sure I do."

"Then shut your trap and listen."

"My mom has taken me out a few times to practice in the Buick."

"This here ain't no old lady's Buick. This here is a finely tuned machine. The slightest pressure on the gas, and we're out of here in a split second. Got it?" Garret said.

I nodded, with more conviction than I felt.

"Now, when I tell you, and not a minute before, I want you to put your right foot on the brake pedal and turn the key in the ignition."

I placed my fingers on the key.

"No, not now. When I tell you!"

"I was just getting the feel of it."

"Now, when this baby turns over, prepare yourself for a rush. It can go to your head pretty darn quick, and I just want you to be aware of what you're doing at all times."

"Sure, sure." I fingered the key. "Now?"

Garret nodded.

"Now."

I turned around once to glance at Jimmy. He was leaning forward and grabbing the back of the front seat, grinning; his head nodded, like a bobblehead doll.

I pressed my foot on the brake pedal and turned the key in the ignition. The engine roared to life. My whole body vibrated with the power at the tip of my toes. I shifted into drive and slowly released the brake. The Chevy rolled forward, and I panicked and slammed my foot on the brake. Garret lurched forward in his seat.

"What the hell are you doing?"

"I panicked."

"You know what to expect now. Try again."

I tightened my grip on the wheel, looked both ways, and lifted my foot off the brake. The car rolled forward again, and I applied a bit of pressure on the gas pedal. We shot out into the middle of Ash, and I steered to the left, straightened out, and cruised to South Avenue. At South, I stopped.

"Which way?"

"Left," Garret said.

I turned left and touched the gas pedal again, bringing her up to about thirty-five miles per hour. It felt like we were doing a hundred.

"Turn left at the light," Garret said.

We cruised down Fourth Street toward Grand Avenue, the main cruising route on Friday and Saturday nights. As I pulled to a stop at the red light, a silver and black pickup stopped beside us. Jared, a guy from my class, leaned out the window.

"Hey Dusty! When did you get your license?"

"I . . . I . . ."

"When did they make you a deputy?" Garret hollered back.

The light changed; I waved and pulled away before Jared could ask any more questions. The last thing I wanted to do was get Garret in trouble. He'd kill me.

For awhile, we just rode around, up and down Grand Avenue, over and over again in a big loop, honking at girls in cars, flirting with those who looked interested, ogling those who didn't. We turned it into a game, rating the cruising girls from one to ten, according to a ranking system known only to us. Sitting behind the wheel of Garret's Chevy I was a dude. A hunk. A man. I was tough. And the girls couldn't take their eyes off of me.

"I've got to take a leak," Garret said.

"We could stop at the fire station," Jimmy said.

"Nah. Turn right on Fifth," Garret said.

"Where are we going?"

"You'll see. When we get down to Oklahoma Avenue turn right, and I'll tell you where to stop."

I turned on Oklahoma Avenue and drove slow waiting for Garret to give the word. Before he could, I heard a commotion in the backseat.

"This is Stephen Crazy Arrow's house," Jimmy said.

"I know that," Garret said.

He climbed out of the car and walked to a tree in the front yard of Stephen's house. Garret glanced from side to side, unzipped his pants, and proceeded to pee on the tree.

Before Jimmy or I could respond, I heard the front door of the house squeak open, and Mr. Crazy Arrow came out on his porch.

"Hey boy, go somewhere else and do that!" he yelled at Garret.

"It's a free country!" Garret hollered back. "And don't call me 'boy,' red man."

"The name's Crazy Arrow."

Mr. Crazy Arrow stepped off his narrow front porch.

"I don't want any trouble."

"Too late," Garret said.

He'd zipped up his pants by now, and I saw him slip his switchblade out of his pocket. He flicked it open and held it up, waving it at Mr. Crazy Arrow. Jimmy and I stared in disbelief as Garret moved closer to our classmate's father.

"Do I need to call the police?" Mr. Crazy Arrow said.

The street light was shining on them, as they faced off. Garret had that fearless look in his eyes.

"Nobody's stopping you," he said, "but they ain't about to help the likes of you."

"Look, son, I think you've had too much to drink. Why don't you go on home and sleep it off," Mr. Crazy Arrow said.

He stepped closer to Garret—his arms outstretched in a fatherly way. He reached out his hand.

"Give me the knife and I won't call the police."

Garret lunged at him. I heard Mr. Crazy Arrow groan and watched him fall backwards onto the ground. He had a hold of Garret's shirt and Garret fell on top of him. They rolled in the grass until Mr. Crazy Arrow landed on top. He scrambled to his feet. The light glanced off the blade of Garret's knife as he tackled Mr. Crazy Arrow again.

Before Jimmy or I could do anything, Mrs. Crazy Arrow came running across the front yard, screaming. She jumped on Garret's back, clawing at his face. Garret released Mr. Crazy Arrow, and Mr. Crazy Arrow fell in a heap on the ground, clutching his belly. Garret pried Mrs. Crazy Arrow's fingers out of his eyes, then spun, trying to throw her off his back. She clung to him, her screams piercing the quiet of the night. Garret twisted hard one more time, and Mrs. Crazy Arrow lost her grip. She fell to the ground with a thump.

In the distance I heard sirens. My whole body trembled. Garret jumped into the front passenger seat of the car.

I glanced back at the Crazy Arrow's house one more time, trying to understand what had just happened. Mr. Crazy Arrow lay still on the ground. Mrs. Crazy Arrow knelt beside him, rocking back and forth, wailing. Through the front window of the house, I saw Stephen peering out between the curtains. His terror-filled gaze held mine.

"Get out of here!" Garret said, his voice hoarse, breathing hard. Blood stained his hands. I shifted into drive and hit the gas. The tires squealed as the car responded, as if it were on automatic pilot.

I don't remember driving out of town. I was numb, clutching the steering wheel as though it were a lifeline. Garret said he was bleeding; Jimmy handed him a rag from under the seat. Garret wrapped it around his injured hand.

My mind raced with wild images of being chased by police cars with their lights flashing and sirens blaring, a chopper circling overhead with its spotlights directed on the top of the Chevy. I couldn't stop glancing in the rearview mirror, but each time the road behind us remained empty.

My knuckles grew sore from gripping the steering wheel so tightly, and I wasn't sure if I'd be able to stand on my legs if called upon to do so. The muscles of my thighs twitched. My stomach felt as though I'd swallowed concrete. My only thought was, *What made Garret attack Mr. Crazy Arrow?*

I think it was at that moment that I realized how hate could take over the mind. Once the mind is convinced, the body reacts and spins out of control, like a race car that can't make a turn. The driver may be holding the steering wheel, but forward momentum takes over, propelling the car over the wall, heedless of what may be in its path—until it hits a tree or wall strong enough to stop it. That is what happened to Garret and it scared me. It scared me real bad.

No one had spoken since we pulled away from Mr. Crazy Arrow's house, and now we were at the Tonkawa city limits, fifteen miles west of Ponca City. Garret told me to pull into a gas station. I turned into the next one, and he jumped out of the car and headed for the men's room. I turned off the engine. I looked at Jimmy in the rearview mirror. Jimmy looked at me. His eyes were round as pancakes. He was trembling.

Garret came back to the car with his hand wrapped in paper towels. Jimmy stared out the window. I saw a tear fall from his cheek. Garret opened the door on the driver's side.

"Move over."

I slid across the seat, and he got in behind the wheel.

"We better not go back to Ponca tonight," Garret said.

He started the car and pulled onto the road, heading for Tonkawa.

"What are we going to do?" I asked.

"We'll lay low for now. In a few days, everything will calm down."

"Yeah, but the police will be looking for us."

"I wouldn't worry too much about that. Indians know better than to point their finger at a white boy."

"Yeah, but what if Mr. Crazy Arrow was hurt?"

"So?" Garret said. "He had it coming. Besides, we're in this together now."

"Hold on," I said. "I didn't do anything."

"You were driving, weren't you? You're an accomplice. That is, you would be if we had committed a crime."

"Assault is a crime," I said.

"Not if it's an Indian. They're used to it. Besides, they cut each other all the time and nobody calls the police. They settle it themselves."

"I don't know," I said.

"Oh, I forgot. Your girlfriend is an Indian-lover."

"Jenna?"

"I saw her sitting with them Indians at the statue."

"So?"

"She's filled your head with that crap about Indian's rights. Maybe you think you're better than me."

"I never said that."

"You, with your fancy house and cheerleader sister. Talking French and taking geometry. You've looked down your nose at me since first grade."

"That's not true," I said. "Let's just go home and explain what happened. We'll say that we thought we had a flat tire, and when we stopped to look at it, Mr. Crazy Arrow came out and threatened us. I saw a broom on the front porch. We could say he threatened us with it. It's our word against theirs. Right, Jimmy?"

Jimmy stared out the window. He didn't say a word.

By now, I realized Garret had driven through Tonkawa. We were past the city limits of the town and back in the country. No street lights out this far and not much traffic. The full moon illuminated acres of wheat fields, which stretched for miles and miles on both sides of the road.

Garret pulled the car over onto the shoulder of the road and got out. He walked around to the edge of the shoulder, turned his back to us, unzipped his pants, and sprayed pee across the rocky ditch. When he returned to the car, he opened my door and pulled me out by my arm.

"Hey! What are you doing," I said.

"You want to go home? Go ahead."

He slammed my door closed.

"Quit your fooling," I said. "You can't leave me out here in the middle of nowhere."

I reached for the door handle.

Garret slammed his fist into my gut. The air rushed out of me and I couldn't draw in a breath. He grabbed my arm and twisted it behind me.

"Indian-lovers end up like them, in the ditch."

Out of the darkness I heard a scream. Garret heard it, too, because he stopped talking and looked up and down the road. At first

I thought it was a police siren, but then I saw the broad wingspan of the white eagle.

It swooped down toward our heads; its sharp claws extended, as though its prey was in reach. Garret ducked his head and shoved me hard from behind. I fell head first into the ditch. Pain exploded in my forehead as my head bounced off a jagged rock. My body flipped over. When I landed, my arm lay at a funny angle, but I felt no pain. I heard the Chevy start up; its rear tires pummeled me with gravel as my friends pulled onto the road.

The last thing I remember before I blacked out was the massive white eagle circling above me, claws extended, reaching for the kill.

SEVEN

HOW MUCH FARTHER? How much longer do we have to walk?" It was me talking, but my voice disappeared into the vastness of the desolate, rolling prairie, smothered by the driving rain that soaked through every thread covering my body. I shivered. The waterlogged weight on my back had grown too much to bear. The muddy cloths wrapping my feet were now rags, flapping against my legs with each step I took.

The bundle on my back shifted. A frail voice spoke.

"I'm hungry."

It was Stephanie's voice, weak and broken, not the loud and happy voice of Stephanie on the swing set or greeting me at the door at home. No doors here, only endless snow-covered fields stretching seemingly without end.

A leather pouch hung from my neck. I opened it and pulled out a piece of what appeared to be dried meat.

"Chew on this," I told her.

It wasn't much. And though I had no idea where I was or why

she sounded so weak, somehow I knew it would not be enough to fill her stomach. Her legs were wrapped around me, and the rags on her feet were black from dried blood, blood from the wounds of walking too many miles with only scraps of cloth to serve as shoes. She took the meat from my hand, her fingers feeble, yet with a desperate determination.

Up ahead, I saw my mother trod over the rocky path, her footing unsure on the slick surfaces, my father five steps ahead of her. And in front of my father, hundreds of people, like us, their bare heads lowered and turned against the harsh winds and pelting rain, a hopelessness all but visible in their steps. I felt the aching of their souls. Hope had been vanquished, as they marched in endless steps across an endless land.

A breath. A whimper. Silence. A tiny hand dropped to my shoulder and hung there, swinging in rhythm with my steps. Rivulets of rainwater coursed across the feathery hairs on her arm. Gripped by fear, pain, terror, I took Stephanie's hand in my own, if for no other reason than to keep it from bumping against my shoulder. The skin was cold. The bones fine. Lifeless.

I screamed my anger to the howling wind; my pain tore through me, like a knife.

My mother stopped.

One glance at my face told the story. She fell to the ground, pounded her fists, pulled her hair in grief. Her wails halted the march. My father ran towards me, his face growing older with each of the few steps it took to reach me. Rain beat down on his head, streamed from the tips of his braids. He understood instantly. His grief evident in his eyes, as he bore down on me, piercing me with a look as if he had launched a thousand quills.

"We can't bury her here," he said.

"I'll carry her," I said.

A solemn nod. He lifted my mother to her feet. They again began walking. I followed, my heart as heavy and hidden as the boulders beneath the snow-covered earth. I was in a void, white as a sheet. A man stood in front of me in a light so bright I couldn't make out his features. His arms raised from his sides, like wings, blocking out the light. His face came into focus: Two golden eyes at half-mast, sunken behind high cheekbones, with skin as tough as shoe leather and as wrinkled. A thin stern mouth and a gaze that set my knees to shaking. Long, white braids, wrapped with beaver skins, hung from each shoulder and a bone breastplate covered his chest. Intricate beadwork adorned the white buckskins he wore.

"Who are you?"

"On earth, I was known as Chief White Eagle, main chief of the Poncas."

"Am I dead?"

"That is not for me to answer."

"What am I doing here?"

"When I was a boy, the eagle carried me high in the sky. I learned to see far and wide. To rise above my small world. I am your eagle."

"I don't understand."

Chief White Eagle spread his wings, and we were soaring above the earth dodging dark clouds. Lightning flashed around us lighting the way, like street lamps on a rainy highway. My eyes saw all the nuances of the great plains below. A long black snake moved over the land, stretching across many miles. I saw my mother, my father, me, walking. Walking along with hundreds of others.

"Who are they?" I asked, pointing at the snake.

"They are my people."

"Poncas?"

"Yes."

"Where are they going? Why are they walking?"

"We were forced to leave our homes by the Niobrara River. The government gave our land to the Lakota. My people walked six hundred miles to a land so poor nothing would grow. We were farmers along the Niobrara what you now call Nebraska. We lived in frame homes as the white man did. We never went to war with the white man. We were happy. They took away our tools, our animals, our

hope. One out of three of us died. From sickness. From hunger. From broken hearts."

"I don't want to hear anymore," I said.

The memory of Stephanie lifeless on my back made my chest ache. I remembered the pain on my mother's face, the empty gaze of my father. But he continued.

"The plants were different in this new land. We didn't know which plants to use for medicine. We had no clothing fit for the cold wet winters. Two winters came and went, and we became desperate. More died. From bad water. The ground would not yield crops to sustain us. We were a broken people.

"Then Chief Standing Bear's son died. It was a sad day. He had lost his daughter, Prairie Flower, on the walk down to Indian Territory. Standing Bear promised his son that should he die that the boy would be buried with the old people along the Niobrara. Standing Bear was a man of his word.

"A party of thirty Poncas, led by Standing Bear, left in the dead of winter. They walked for two months. They were often cold and often hungry. They had the bones of Standing Bear's son with them. They were arrested at the Omaha reservation. Standing Bear sued the government for wrongful imprisonment, but, according to the white man's law, Indians were as children in the eyes of the government and could not bring suit against it."

"What happened?" I asked.

A whirlwind of color and sound surrounded me. People crying, people starving, people whirling in a huge tornado with me at its center. I became dizzy with emotion, my eyes swimming in my head, until finally I lost my bearing.

Then, as suddenly, stillness.

I found myself sitting in an circa-1880s courtroom full of Indians, whites, lawyers, and military guards. Standing room only. Up in front of the railing that divided the spectators from the court proceedings, I saw a statuesque Indian. He wore a magnificent feather in his long hair. On one side of his head his hair hung straight; on the other, a braid was wrapped with beaver fur. A red blanket trimmed with broad blue stripes draped one shoulder and wrapped around his torso, secured at his waistline with a wide beaded belt. He wore a necklace of bear claws. In his hand, an eagle feather fan.

His presence hushed the crowd.

"Your honor, if it would please the court, Standing Bear would like to speak on his own behalf. Mr. Willie W. Hamilton has agreed to interpret for the court."

"Proceed."

Standing Bear removed his blanket, handing it to a woman sitting behind him. He looked at her for a long moment, their eyes communicating an unspoken solidarity, before he turned to face the judge. He spoke in the language of the Ponca. Mr. Hamilton translated his words into English.

"From the time I went down to Indian Territory until I left, one-hundred and fifty-eight of us died. I thought to myself, *God wants me to live, and I think if I come back to my old reservation he will let me live.*

"I got back as far as the Omahas, and they brought me down here. I see you all today. What have I done? I am brought here, but what have I done? I don't know.

"I only wanted to go on my own land that has always been mine. I never sold it. That is where I wanted to go. When my son died, I promised him that if I ever returned home that I would take his bones there and bury him. I have my son's bones in a box with me. If I ever go there, I will bury him. That is where I want to live and that is where I want to die.

"You say we are children in the eyes of the law.

"Then I say the law is a child."

He held out his hand before the judge.

"My hand is not the color of yours, but if I pierce it, I shall feel pain. If you pierce yours, you also feel pain. The blood that will flow from mine will be the same color as yours.

"I am a man. The same God made us both."

At the end of his short address, people broke into applause.

They encircled the chief, shaking his hand, offering support, and wishing him well.

I was awed by the man's eloquence, for that is what he was, a man, in the truest sense of the word. In that moment, I realized there was much I did not understand and had not been taught during my fifteen-and-a-half years of life in Ponca City. But before I could make sense of the implications of the chief's testimony and the crowd's response, without warning, I was whisked away into the white void once more.

Chief White Eagle stood before me.

"When I was a boy, I was a bear, standing alone. I learned to look inside myself."

"You mean like Standing Bear at the trial."

"Yes."

"He wasn't afraid to stand up for what he knew was right."

"Yes."

"But how do you know what is right?"

"You must be like the bear."

"I'm confused," I said.

Chief White Eagle was talking in circles, in meanings that were foreign to me. A new kind of parable.

"There is more to see," he said.

Chief White Eagle spread his wings. I closed my eyes, afraid to look at what was to come next.

A gale wind engulfed me, its roar deafening in my ears, its force cutting, as if razor blades were being sharpened on my skin. I opened my eyes and saw we flew at treetop level, the tips of the trees were the razor blades I felt. I hung from the white eagle's talons.

Eventually, he lowered me onto the topmost branch of a pecan tree, then came to rest beside me. I heard a scream and looked down. Huddled at the base of the tree was a young girl. She looked exactly like Jenna. And she looked to be hiding as well, until two uniformed men spotted her, grabbed her, and dragged her away.

"Jenna," I called out, but she was too far away.

"Where are they taking her?" I asked.

The white eagle spread his wings, and I found myself whisked once more above the treetops, following the path the two men had taken. The men had dragged Jenna through the undergrowth past a house at the edge of the woods. Mrs. Marker was crying, pleading with them not to take her daughter away. The two men shoved Jenna into the back of their car and drove off; the spinning wheels of the car filled the road behind them with dust. We soared above the road, following them. The men drove into Ponca City, but it looked different. Fewer houses and no refinery on the south end of town. *What year was this?* I wondered.

The policemen drove to the railroad station on Fourth Street and got out of the car. They dragged Jenna from the back seat and roughly pushed her towards a waiting boxcar. One of the officers held onto Jenna, while the other opened the sliding door. Inside the boxcar were a dozen others. Some crying. Others huddled against the sides.

"What are they doing with those kids?" I asked.

Soon the boxcar was locked, and the train pulled out. The white eagle carried me for many miles, high above the clouds, until he set me down on a campanile. The bell inside swung slowly to and fro; its ringing vibrated my whole being and filled my ears with melancholic tones.

The white eagle came to rest in the top of a towering evergreen. It was the tallest tree I'd ever seen, nestled in a grove that surrounded the schoolyard. So intent on his position was I, that I lost my hold on the steep roof and slid down, down, down, unable to regain my grip. I landed flat on my back in the soft green grass of the schoolyard.

The next thing I heard was an authoritative voice behind me; before I could turn or run, I was brought to my feet and spun around nose to nose with a stern woman in a coarse, brown high-collared dress and black, buttoned boots. Her face was pinched into a frown of prune proportions.

"Just what did you think you were doing? Sabotaging the campanile? Think you're going to escape from the roof, do you? What are you a bird? And on your first day, yet. Well, I can tell you're going to be trouble. We'll take care of that this minute. Three days in the basement ought to set you straight."

She hauled me off by the arm to a small building adjacent to the schoolhouse. She opened the heavy wooden door and thrust me inside ahead of her. The room was barren of any rugs, wall ornaments, or furniture, save for a few spindly chairs.

Seated on one of the chairs was Jenna. She sat with her head down. As I was pushed down onto the chair opposite her, she did not throw so much as a glance in my direction. Behind her a matronly woman sharpened a razor on a leather strap. Turning once more to stand behind Jenna, the woman swept up Jenna's braid and whacked it off at her neck.

"This one is next," said the woman in brown, "then to the basement with him."

"Yes, ma'am," the barber said.

Jenna's eyes met mine with a flicker of recognition.

"Where are we?" I asked in a language I didn't know.

"Carlisle, Pennsylvania," Jenna said in the same language.

With a great rage, the barber threw down her razor, grabbed the leather strap with one hand, and upturned Jenna and her chair with the other. Jenna fell to the floor.

"English is the only language spoken here," the barber shouted.

With that, she began to strike Jenna across her back with the leather strap. Jenna cried out in pain at first, until the pain grew so great that all she could do was whimper.

"Stop it!" I screamed.

The barber turned her anger then upon me and came at me, strap raised above her head, preparing to strike me as well. In trying to escape her wrath, my chair fell over backwards and dumped me in a heap on the floor. She had me trapped.

The stinging blows of the leather strap bore down on my flesh, but I refused to cry out in pain, and that led the barber to set her jaw in such a way as to bite me in two pieces. She grabbed me by my arm, took up Jenna with her other hand, and marched us unceremoniously out the door, across the yard, and down a set of stairs that led below the grand colonial house opposite the schoolhouse. With one mighty shove, Jenna and I found ourselves alone on the dirt floor of the cavernous basement.

Fragmented light seeped in through narrow gaps between the boards of the door. A few minutes passed before our eyes adjusted to the darkness. I could make out the shape of Jenna's face, but her features remained shadowed. She spoke to me in the same strange language again.

"You are Ponca."

"Yes," I said.

"Why are we here?" I asked in her language.

"To become white."

"But we are Ponca. How can we become white?"

"They want us to speak as the white man, dress as the white man."

She paused. I could not see her eyes, but I sensed the bitterness in her words.

"They cannot make us think as the white man."

"What will happen now?"

"We must stay here for a long time, until our people no longer know us. The white man is blinded by our color. He does not see that we are human beings. He does not see our wisdom. He does not see into our hearts. I have heard stories of those who went before me to Indian school and returned. They cannot find a home in either world."

We spoke of many things during our incarceration. I listened to her words, digested her thoughts, tasted the salt from her tears. Three days passed, as promised, before our release.

When the door to our prison was finally unbarred by the guard, the bright sunshine slashed across our faces and seared our eyes.

Almost blinded, we were led to separate dormitories. It was a painful parting. Jenna and I had forged a bond that neither time nor space could erase.

The white void enveloped me again.

Chief White Eagle appeared in front of me.

"When I was a boy, I was a buffalo. I learned there is a time to be quiet. I did not speak of what I had heard. A wise man speaks few words."

"You've lost me," I said. "What does keeping quiet have to do with Jenna."

"That is not for me to answer."

"I am totally confused. When can I go home? I don't want to see any more. I don't want to feel any more pain. My heart is torn in two. I want to go home."

"There is more to see."

The white eagle spread his wings.

We circled high above the earth. The sun blinded my eyes. Its heat intense. The eagle's talons dug into my shoulders. Slowly, slowly, we neared the ground; once more I could see my home. My heart ached to be with Stephanie, to hug her warm body close to me, to see my mother and father, to hear Jenna's sweet voice once more.

I found myself in a parking lot full of cars. Tepees and tarpaulins dotted the grass. Past the parking lot, flood lights spotlighted an arena. A stream of people carrying folding chairs, picnic baskets, ice chests, and blankets filled the center drive that led to the arena. Some men carried suitcases. A gentle shove from behind set my feet in motion.

"Okay. I'm going," I said to the white eagle.

I took my time crossing the parking lot and fell in back of the line slowly threading its way to the gathering place.

The rhythm of the drum pounded, giving life to the darkness. Around the arena, people sat in folding chairs in their chosen spaces. Babies played on blankets on the ground. Ice chests served as tables. In the center of it all, ten men sat around a massive drum.

Each drummer had long, straight black hair. Each beat the same drum with wood-and-leather sticks. And as they beat, they chanted melancholy words of warriors lost in battle. Their words were in that strange language again, but somehow I understood. Twenty women in native dress stood or sat around the circle of men. Their voices rose and fell, intoning the songs with the men. A broad expanse of packed dirt separated the drummers and singers from the crowd. Filling that space were dancers—men, women, and children, all wearing buckskin adorned with delicate beadwork, hair ornaments of beaver and otter skins, feathers and ribbons of many colors, and bells of all shapes and sizes. It was a melange of color and sound, all moving to the rhythm of the drum.

When the song ended, the master of ceremonies announced someone had left car lights on in the parking lot and reminded people to keep an eye on their children. Vendors sold cold drinks, fry bread, and toys for the children; artists displayed handmade jewelry and paintings.

I wandered around the outside of the dance circle, weaving between the hundreds of people milling about. It reminded me of an elaborate family reunion. I saw women embracing as though they hadn't seen each other for awhile. Children raced to play their favorite games together, teenagers huddled in groups, and old people sat on their folding chairs absorbing the sights and sounds and smells, reminiscing, gossiping, observing.

Someone called out my name. I turned and saw Leslie Cries For War approaching. He wore regalia bedecked with brightly colored feathers. Black stripes were painted across his broad cheekbones. Sleigh bells lined his legs from the knee down.

"You must dance with us tonight," he said.

"But I'm not dressed for it."

"What you wear is fine."

I glanced down and saw I was wearing a shirt with ribbons, blue jeans, and moccasins. He led me to the circle, and I copied his movements, bending my knees in rhythm with the drum. It soon became easy to stay in step. This close to the drum and the singers, the motion of my body separated from my thoughts. I had become one with the drum. One heartbeat for us all. It was as though I had slipped back in time thousands of years to relive a previous life, back to my origins. The trappings fell away. The endless prairie reclaimed me. Dancing alongside me was Chief White Eagle. His solemn expression unchanged.

"Why are you here with me?" I asked him.

"It has been many winters since I have danced. When I was a boy, I was a mouse. I learned what it was to be insignificant. I took comfort in simple pleasures. Now this is my one pleasure. Everything of importance is found here. It is easy to feel lost in the wide arms of Mother Earth."

"What does it mean? The eagle, the bear, the buffalo, the mouse? What does it have to do with me?"

"That is not for me to answer. Each man must decide for himself."

The drum stilled.

Chief White Eagle faded away.

"Don't go!" I yelled.

I had many more questions. Many things I didn't understand.

My eyes became heavy with sleep.

Eight

WHEN MY EYES OPENED AGAIN of their own volition, I was in bed. A hospital bed. A wave of panic coursed through my body. What had happened to me? Why was I here? My forehead itched, but my left arm was too heavy to raise it to scratch. A plaster cast encased my arm from above my elbow down to the tips of my fingers. I tried my right hand. A tube was plugged into a needle lodged in my forearm. I reached for my forehead. It was wrapped in gauze and tape. Trying to scratch where the itch was did no good, because the bandage was too thick to make satisfactory contact.

My eyelashes were pressed against my lids. When I ran my fingers across them, they felt spongy, swollen, and sore. The muscles in my shoulders and back hurt, too, as though I'd been carrying sacks of flour for hours.

As for my head, well, it felt like the entire Ponca High marching band was stomping through it. But it was my bladder that made me move. I had to go, bad. I swung my legs off the side of the bed and slid my bottom to the edge just as a nurse came through the door. Her brown eyes flared at the sight of me moving.

"Need some help?" she asked.

Her thin frame belied her strength, for she was at my side in two steps, taking my arm firmly in her grasp. She rolled the IV alongside as we made our way to the bathroom.

"What day is this?" I asked.

"Monday."

"How long have I been here?"

"They brought you in yesterday."

"Who?"

"First things first."

She opened the bathroom door and flipped on the light switch.

"I can manage from here," I said.

"Are you sure?"

I nodded, automatically. My head throbbed.

"I'll be right outside the door if you need help," she said.

She wheeled the IV trolley into the bathroom with me and closed the door. I turned around and came face to face with the mirror over the sink. Wow! My eyes peered back at me out of a black and blue mask beneath the white turban bandage. My eyelids both bulged out and hung down part way over my eyes. It was the face of an alien. I ran my fingers over the discolored skin. Not only did my head ache, but my skin was sensitive to the touch.

When I came out, my bladder was the only part of my body that felt better. The nurse took my arm and the IV trolley once more and walked with me back to the bed.

"I imagine you're hungry," she said, tucking the sheet and blanket around my legs. "I'll see if I can round up a tray for you."

I hadn't thought about food until she mentioned it, but she was right. I was starving.

"Just push this button here if you need anything. I'll be right back."

The nurse call button and the television controls were in one remote control unit, hung on the rail of the bed. The very idea of turning on the television made my head hurt more, if that was possible. A soft rap on wood, followed by a slowly opening door revealed my mother. Her face was ashen, a weak smile contradicted by the tears in her eyes. My own eyes watered at the sight of her.

"We've been so worried about you," she said.

We wrapped arms around each other as best we could. I could tell she was afraid of causing me more pain, but I didn't care. I needed my mother to hug me. I held on for a long time.

Then my father was standing bedside. I can't remember the last time I'd seen him cry. But he was now. So was I. We embraced each other as though nothing would separate us ever again.

"You caused your mother quite a scare," he said, easing out of my grasp.

A niggling thought pushed its way to the front of my thoughts.

"I was wondering . . . I was wondering about Stephanie. Is she all right?" I asked.

"She's fine," my father said. "She's been worried about you, though. Funny thing, she woke up Saturday night screaming from a bad nightmare. It took us almost an hour to get her back to sleep. She had dreamed that . . ."

"I don't think he needs to hear all of that right now," my mother said.

Her face had taken on a pained expression at the thought of whatever Stephanie had dreamt. When had I ever seen her face so drawn? A panorama rolled through my mind, disjointed and jumbled together as though someone who'd never seen the whole picture had found it cut into small pieces, then tried to fit it back together again.

A tall, gray-haired man wearing a white lab coat came through the door and the image in my mind disappeared. His smile spoke volumes.

"So, young man, you're back among the living," he said. "I'm Doctor Kirkendall."

My father swiped at his eyes and stepped awkwardly away from the bed as though he didn't know whether to sit down or stand along the wall. My mother pointed at the chair next to hers.

"Your mother and father have kept quite a vigil over you," Dr. Kirkendall said, "but I must say I've never seen two people more positive in their outlook. Let me have a look at you."

Dr. Kirkendall shone a light into my eyes, checked my pulse, listened to my heart.

"The nurse told me you're hungry. That's a very good sign. I think we can safely remove that tube now. We're going to move you out of Intensive Care, but I'd like to keep you a few more days for observation," he threw a glance in the direction of my parents. "If that's all right with you two?"

They nodded.

"We feel that is sensible," my father said, "after what he's been through."

"Good. I'll make the arrangements to have you moved today."

Intensive Care? Me? The shock must have registered on my face.

"What's wrong, Dusty?" my mother asked.

The doctor looked up from his clipboard.

"I just don't remember what happened."

"It may take a few days for your memory to return," Dr. Kirkendall said. "You suffered a blow to the head, a concussion to be exact, quite severe actually. You were unconscious when they brought you in. You also suffered a fractured elbow. That, I'm afraid, is going to take more than a few days to heal. But we can talk more about that later."

"How long am I going to look like . . . like this?"

"The swelling has already gone down some," Dr. Kirkendall said. "The discoloration will fade over the next few weeks."

"Weeks? Am I going to have to go to school like this?" I asked.

"The bruises will probably be gone by the time you return to school," Dr. Kirkendall said.

I stared at him dumbfounded. Then I smiled.

"That's the best news I've heard," I said.

"I'm sure we can find a tutor to keep you up on your schoolwork during your confinement," my father said.

"Oh."

The nurse came in with a tray and set it on the table.

"I see your lunch is here," said Dr. Kirkendall. "Glad to see you've come out of it so quickly. You're one of the lucky ones. Well, *bon appétit!*"

Dr. Kirkendall started to walk out of the room, only to pause and turn back to face my parents.

"The police indicated they would like to speak with Dusty," he said. "I informed them that they'd have to discuss it with you, but my opinion is that it should wait a few days, until his thinking clears."

Tears of gratitude welled up in my mother's eyes.

"Thank you, doctor."

Dr. Kirkendall gave my mother a quick hug.

"You've been brave through all of this. Both of you."

He reached out and patted my father's arm. Before leaving, he turned to the nurse and instructed her to remove the IV. She did so without pause and then left. With the tube gone from my arm, I felt more like eating. My nurse must have read my mind, because she rolled back through the door with a cart of food. She parked the table close so I could reach it.

"It's the best I could do," she said, "between shifts."

I lifted the domed cover from the plate.

"A cheeseburger and fries?" I said.

"Your dad brought it, just in case you woke up and were hungry," the nurse said, smiling with a glance in my father's direction. "I reheated it in the microwave. I hope it's not too soggy."

"It's perfect," I said.

I tried to pick up the burger with my one able hand, but it started coming apart. "This is going to be tricky."

My mother came to the rescue. She cut the burger in half so I could manage it by myself. She must have realized that I'd balk at the idea of her trying to feed me. *How did she know these things?*

70

After I'd eaten every last French fry, I found my head didn't hurt as much, but I was tired as I'd ever been. I lay back on the pillow. No one had mentioned anything about how I had gotten to the hospital. I remained foggy on the happenings of the past few days. I remembered being excited about the town's centennial celebration, but I couldn't remember any details about it.

"I missed the whole weekend," I said.

My father shifted uneasily on his chair, while my mother played with the buttons on her blouse.

"Did I say something wrong?" I asked.

"Oh no, dear," my mother said. "I just think it would be better if you didn't worry yourself about that right now. You need your rest."

"The nurse said someone brought me in yesterday."

"Yes, that's true," my mother said.

"Why do the police want to talk to me?"

"Dusty, I think your mother has been through enough. She's been here all night, worried sick that you wouldn't—."

Their gazes met, a consensus struck.

"Anyway, there is plenty of time for questions, later," my father said. "Right now, you look tired."

"But I slept for more than twenty-four hours, and I can't remember what happened."

I was getting riled. Didn't I have a right to know what had happened to me? Before I could protest anymore, the nurse returned with a tray. It held a tiny paper cup with a pill in it.

"The doctor prescribed this for pain," the nurse said.

"I'm feeling better."

"Maybe you should take it." My mother said as she glanced knowingly at the nurse. "It will help you to relax."

I put the pill on the back of my tongue and took a long drink of water. Maybe she was right. I was too tense. But didn't I have a good reason to be?

My parents sat with me for awhile, waiting for the pill to do its job before they left for home.

71

"We'll come back in a bit, Dusty. If you need anything at all, call me at home," my mother said, fluffing my pillow. "And if you start feeling worse, the nurses are right outside. Don't be afraid to call them."

"Okay, Mom," I said. "And Mom . . ."

"Yes dear?"

"It's been a long time since I've told you how much I love you." She smiled bigger than ever and patted my hand.

"I love you, too." She hugged me again. "I'll be back shortly."

"You get some rest now, son," my father said.

He waved to me from the door, then followed my mother out.

I dozed on and off for a few hours after they left. I couldn't help wondering what had happened to land me in the hospital with a broken elbow and a concussion. My body hurt as though I'd walked for miles. Walking for miles. Why did I think that? If anything, I would have run, not walked. Walking is so boring. I needed to get out of this bed. My bottom was sore from laying down, and I was beginning to feel penned in. I sat up, allowing the throbbing to subside before edging off the bed. My feet hurt, too. My slippers were on the floor. I slid my feet into them. I picked up the robe my mother had laid across the end of the bed and discovered it had been de-sleeved on the left side. It made me laugh to see my robe with only one sleeve. And it made me feel warm inside to know that my mother had done it for me. Mother wasn't the type to fuss over us. But when it came to important matters, she was always there.

As I tried to maneuver my immobile, tripled-sized left arm through the armhole of my robe, the door to my room opened. It was my nurse again, pushing a wheelchair.

"Moving day," the nurse said. "I take it you're ready to get out of here and into a regular room?"

"You bet."

She began collecting the few possessions I had from the narrow closet and put them in a duffle bag. She patted the seat of the wheelchair. "Hospital policy," she said.

I lowered myself into the wheelchair, and she plopped the duffle bag on my lap. She pushed me out into the hallway, onto the elevator, up one floor, off the elevator, and down the hall to my new room. It took all of five minutes but it left me exhausted. I couldn't wait to climb back into bed and lay down.

Of the two beds in the room, I chose the one closest to the window. The other was unoccupied. I had just stretched out and closed my eyes when I heard someone enter the room. It was a hospital volunteer wheeling a small cart; I recognized her as a customer at my father's grocery store. Mrs. Pendergrass, if I remembered correctly.

"How are we feeling, Dusty?" she said in her singsong voice. "I was shocked to hear what that Indian did to you. Oh, and your poor mother. She's been soooo upset about the whole scandal."

"Thank you for asking, Mrs. Pendergrass. I'm much better—"

"The whole city is buzzing with it. Why, just this morning I overheard someone talking about how the mayor wasn't going to stand for this type of violence in our fair city. How's she going to stop those Indians from coming into town? They're the root of all this barbaric behavior, if you ask me."

Her words ignited feelings of anger in me that I'd never known I could harbor. Before I could stop myself, I said, "They were here first." *Did I just say that?*

Mrs. Pendergrass' mouth dropped open. Her double chin folded into tiny pleats. Nothing came out of the space between her nose and bottom lip. She couldn't seem to decide whether she should stay or leave, but she was speechless, for once in her life.

When she finally spoke her words came out short, choppy.

"Do you want a newspaper or not?"

"Yes, thank you."

She threw the paper onto my bed and backed her cart out of the room, muttering about water on the brain and me being hit on the head too hard. I heard her enter the room across the hall already recovered, announcing in that singsong voice, "You won't believe what the Hamilton boy just said to me!"

73

Was I crazy? Of all people to make such a comment to, I say it to Mrs. Pendergrass? Her reputation for volunteer work was second only to her penchant for repeating everything she hears, sees, smells, tastes, touches, or happens to fall over. How many times had I heard my mother tell Mrs. Marker in one of their phone calls (telephone-marathons is what my dad and I called them) that if you wanted to know something, ask Mrs. Pendergrass. But water it down first, she'd warn.

I grabbed the newspaper from the end of my bed and scanned the front page, my mind reeling from our brief exchange. I leafed through the pages, searching for the comic strips, anything to divert my attention from what had just happened.

On one of the last pages of the newspaper, a headline grabbed my attention.

CRAZY ARROW'S ASSAILANT ARRESTED

PONCA CITY, Okla.—A local man believed to have assaulted Donald Crazy Arrow at his home Saturday evening was charged with attempted murder after being seen at St. Joseph Hospital, Sunday morning. Eighteen-year-old Leslie Cries For War of Ponca City was reportedly seen leaving the emergency room early Sunday; police picked him up after a positive identification was made by a hospital employee.

The employee, who preferred to remain nameless, says Cries For War told him he had found a 15-year-old Ponca City boy unconscious alongside the road outside Tonkawa and brought him to the hospital for treatment. Police officials believe Cries For War is responsible not only for the assault on Crazy Arrow and his wife earlier that evening but also for the one on the 15-year-old.

As of Monday morning, Crazy Arrow remains in critical condition at St. Joseph's Hospital. His wife, who received cuts and bruises in an effort to stop her husband's assailant, was treated and released. At press time the 15-year-old boy was reported to be in a coma at the hospital.

74

I couldn't believe what I was reading. It flipped a switch on in my head, and a movie began playing out in my mind. I began to remember. I was driving Garret's Chevy. Garret holding his knife. Mr. Crazy Arrow on the ground. His wife kneeling beside him. Her helpless cries. Jimmy in the back seat. Stephen in the window. Yes, yes, it was all coming back to me now. Garret's hand wrapped in a bloody rag. Driving out of Tonkawa, pulling to the side of the road. Garret peeing in the ditch. His fist in my gut. Gasping for air. The push. Falling head first. The white eagle's claws.

My head began to throb. I pushed the nurse call button on the bed rail.

"Yes?"

"My head hurts."

"I'll be right there."

A different nurse, one who wore her strength in the set of her jaw and ball-bearing-gray eyes, came through the doorway with a tray in her plump hand. Her gray hair was short and thin and stuck out from her head as though she'd eaten too many jalapeno peppers or stuck her finger in a light socket. Without a word, she thrust the tray towards me. I knew the routine by now. I picked up the small paper cup and swallowed the tiny pill with a gulp of water.

"Thanks," I said.

"Uh-huh."

She strode out of the room, pulling the door nearly closed.

I lay my head back on the pillow and tried not to think about anything, waiting for the medicine to kick in. In particular, I tried not to think what would happen if I told the police what I knew about Saturday night and how Mr. Cries For War had been hurt.

For a brief second, I wished I was still in a coma. I hated to think about what Garret would do to me if I were to tell the truth.

But what might happen to Leslie Cries For War, if I didn't?

NINE

THE PAIN PILL RELIEVED the throbbing in my head, but it did nothing to help me sleep. I was feeling more relaxed, though my fear and confusion made me long for the clock to be turned back. What though would I have done differently?

I had looked forward to and schemed right along with Garret and Jimmy, planning the entire weekend of freedom. Freedom from school, freedom from work, freedom from parental rule. How I had anticipated those forty-eight hours of freedom and celebrating.

When I thought about turning fifteen, I imagined it as endless days of hanging with my buddies, cruising the town on Saturday nights. I couldn't wait to take driver's education, get my learner's permit, and earn my driver's license. But my fifteenth year was turning out to be nothing like what I had expected. So far it was only more responsibilities, more homework, and more confusion when it came to girls.

And now look at the mess I was in.

The most painful events in life have nothing to do with physical injury, but a broken elbow and a bashed skull rank pretty high on the scale.

I avoided thinking about Garret. My friend, my hombre, my childhood buddy. His betrayal hurt me in places where I'd never known pain before, deep inside. I couldn't fathom how after all these years of friendship Garret could treat me as though I were a sack of garbage or worse—punching me and leaving me alone in a ditch. We'd had fights before. Knock down, drag out fights that left us both bloodied and bruised. But once we'd gotten the bad blood out of our systems, it was always over and done with. We moved on. No grudges held. No resentment.

But not this time. This time he'd left me. Left me to die on the side of the road. I wiped at the tears streaming down my cheeks and onto the sheet. I was glad no one was around to see me blubbering. Jimmy popped into my mind, and I wondered if Garret had turned on him, as well. Maybe Jimmy had enough smarts to keep his mouth shut, especially after what happened to me. Garret probably talked Jimmy into backing up his story, too. That would explain why the police had arrested Leslie Cries For War. The guy who saved my life. *An Indian had saved my life. And Garret had turned his back on me.*

More tears. I couldn't hold back the sobs. They came in torrents, like rapids, racking my bruised body, restricting my chest until I gasped for breath.

What was I going to do? If I told the truth I might as well kiss my friendship with Garret good-bye. There would be no chance of reconciliation. He would shun me. And this was a small town. He would get everyone else on his side and I'd be alone, banished from ever showing my face at the Fun Zone again.

I wasn't even sure if the police would believe me. What if I told them an Indian saved my life and I was laughed out of town. People would stop coming to buy their groceries at my father's store. He'd have to file bankruptcy. We'd have to move away from Ponca City and start a new life somewhere where no one knew us.

I shivered at the thought of life gone so wrong.

But could I live with myself knowing that Leslie was in prison for a crime he had nothing to do with? I'd end up tormented by my conscience all my days, like the character in that play we studied at school, *Les Misérables*. I would be emotionally dragged down until I felt nothing, no pain but no happiness either. I'd end up dropping out of school, moving out of my house, and living under a bridge somewhere. I'd have to scavenge for food in dumpsters behind seedy restaurants. My parents would be ashamed of me. My sisters would have nothing to do with me. I'd have no friends, no clothes without holes and tears in them.

Did friendship mean so little to my buddies? I could understand Jimmy's loyalties forcing him to take the safe route. But Garret? Come to think of it, if it hadn't been for that harebrained scheme of his with the firecrackers I wouldn't have lost my bicycle. He was too scared to help me look for it. Afraid of being hauled in by the police. And I took up for him. I was ready to lie to my father and blame it on some faceless, non-existent Indian culprit.

What was I thinking? My sister, Danielle, was in that parade. And my mother and Stephanie were in the crowd. They could have been hurt. And I did nothing to stop Garret, nothing. Heck, I was ready to lie about what happened to Mr. Crazy Arrow to save our necks. Garret called me names. And he beat me up and threw me in a ditch. Some friend.

Tears welled in my eyes once more. I grabbed a box of tissues from the bedside table, pulled out a handful of the scratchy, white tissues, and blew my nose into them.

I don't know how long it took for me to cry myself to sleep. I only know that when I opened my eyes Chief White Eagle was stretched out on the other bed in my hospital room, cleaning his fingernails with a bone knife.

"How did you get in here?" I asked, knowing full well a spirit can pretty much go wherever it pleases.

"How do you sleep on these soft scaffolds?" he asked.

"Why are you here?"

"In winter, when the ground was frozen, my people buried the dead on scaffolds."

"Above ground?" I asked.

"Moccasins made of the skin of the deer were put on their feet, so they might not lose their way but move on safely and be recognized by their own people in the spirit world."

He sat upright and turned toward me. His eyes were the gold of sunlight on a deep pond.

"You were crying."

"Wouldn't you be crying if your best friend turned against you, beat you to a pulp, and left you lying in a ditch?"

"The Ponca people reserve the word *friend* for those who have proven themselves worthy. And they remain friends for life."

"It's different in the white man's world."

"Yes. Friendship means very little in your world."

"That's not entirely true, but it's difficult to know who is a true friend and who isn't. The painful part is discovering that someone you thought was a true friend isn't."

"Perhaps you were too hasty to call this one who turned his back on you a friend."

"We've known each other since first grade."

"As children, we have many lessons to learn. Each must follow his own path. Your heart is heavy with grief. Your eyes are clouded with confusion. Have you forgotten the lesson of the eagle?"

"No." I could still feel the weight of Stephanie's lifeless body on my back.

"You must not think your small world is the only one. There are many circles that make the whole. You must rise above. See far and wide."

Chief White Eagle raised his arms. I climbed onto his back, and we soared once more. We flew a few miles south of Ponca City to the Ponca tribal lands. He lowered me to the ground amidst a scattering of brick one-story houses. Graffiti marred the outside windows; curtains blew through open windows with no screens.

Battered cars were parked in the yard, some up on blocks. We drew near an open window.

"What do you see?" Chief White Eagle asked.

"Can they see me?"

"You are like the wind."

I peered in through the opening. Seated at a table in the modest kitchen were the same old woman and her daughter that I had followed in my father's store. The same two women Leslie Cries For War had been with that day. Mrs. Cries For War sobbed openly. The elder sat hunched over, her leathery face moist from tears. She spoke in Ponca, but I understood what she said.

"I will sell my grandfather's eagle feather fan."

"No." Leslie's mother straightened her back. "I won't allow it. That is sacred. That is all you have left."

"But how will we live otherwise? Leslie is not able to work now. He will lose his job."

"I will get work. We will manage."

"Who will hire you? There is no work here, and no white man will want you on his books. Besides, you cannot earn enough to support us and pay for a lawyer."

"I will pay for my son's lawyer, somehow. He is a good boy. He did not do this crime that they say he did."

I backed away from the window.

"I didn't realize Leslie supported his family. I didn't know that he would lose his job."

"There is more," Chief White Eagle said.

Once more we soared above the clouds, but this time back to the hospital. The Intensive Care Unit. Stephen Crazy Arrow sat in a chair next to his father's hospital bed. Tubes and wires connected Mr. Crazy Arrow to monitors of every variety. Stephen's eyes were red from crying.

"This is my fault, father," Stephen said. "If I had stood up to that bully this never would have happened. I am a coward. I am weak. I am ashamed. Please forgive me. Please live."

Stephen's face dropped into his hands.

"Stephen blames himself for this?"

Chief White Eagle nodded. "What do you think will happen to Stephen if his father dies?"

"His father won't die. He has to live," I said.

I recalled the melodramatic scenarios in which I'd envisioned myself since remembering the night of the attack. Stephen's would be much worse, especially if he were to continue blaming himself for his father's death.

"Tell me. Does he live?"

"That is not for me to answer."

"I'm tired. Take me back to my room. I don't want to see anymore."

I awoke to the sound of people entering my room. Stephanie sat space beside me. She clamored to be up on the bed, but my mother held her back.

"It's all right," I said.

In an instant my sister was beside me, throwing her arms wide to give me a hug. The warmth of her body penetrated my being; I hugged her tightly against me with my good arm. She broke away and leaned back on her knees. With a gentleness that only a child's adoration can evoke, she kissed each of my swollen eyelids.

"All better now?" she said, with innocent hopefulness.

Words caught in my throat. I nodded. She hadn't flinched at the ugly bruises and puffy skin around my eyes. I took her tiny hand in mine and smoothed the feathery hairs on her arm. She giggled at my touch.

My mother lifted her from the bed and set her down on the floor.

"Remember our little talk today, dear?" she said, guiding Stephanie to a chair and pulling from a canvas tote a stack of coloring books and a box of crayons. "It's going to take awhile for Dusty to feel all better."

"But kisses are magic, Mommy."

82

"Yes, they are," I said, with a grin. "I think the swelling has gone down already."

"See?" Stephanie said, the corners of her mouth upturned, delighted with herself. She opened a coloring book on her lap and dumped the box of crayons out on the other chair.

"Your father should be here any minute," my mother said, picking up the tissues strewn about my bed and brushing the wrinkles from the sheet and blanket. "He stopped at the school to pick up your assignments for this week and to arrange for a tutor to start coming to the house next week. Danielle will be coming to visit you as soon as cheerleading practice is over."

"That was some magic you performed on my bathrobe," I said.

My mother's hazel eyes met mine.

"I was wondering if you'd notice." She smiled. "You look more rested."

"I slept a little. But this darn cast is rubbing the skin under my arm raw. And I can't even wiggle my fingers. They feel so useless. I feel so useless."

"I can understand that, but your body needs rest to heal."

My father walked through the door before I could respond. He wore a sour expression.

"What's wrong?" my mother asked.

"Dusty, did you take a banana for lunch last week?"

"I don't remem . . ." The rotten banana. "Oh no."

"Oh yes! I found it, by the way, the hard way. I reached in your locker to take out your notebook and stuck my hand right in that gooey mess."

"I was going to take care of it on Monday."

"Likely story," he said, with mock anger. "Next time, eat it before it turns to jelly, okay?

He smiled.

"Sorry."

"I picked up your assignments. Your teachers asked me to tell you not to worry too much about getting them finished this week.

At least you'll have something to keep your mind occupied."

If they only knew just how occupied my mind was, I thought.

The lines in my father's forehead wrinkled.

"Well anyway," he said, "I'm starving."

I'm not sure what caused him to radically change the subject, but I'm glad he did. I was doing everything in my power to remain upbeat and avoid any possibility of in-depth discussion. I wasn't confident that I'd be able to keep my emotions in check, and I wasn't ready to spill my guts to anybody, especially my father. I'd gotten myself into this mess and I had to work it out for myself. Lives were at stake.

When the nurse brought my supper tray into the room and set it on the table, my mother gathered Stephanie's crayons and coloring books and put them back in the canvas bag. My father said he couldn't imagine what was keeping Danielle so long.

"She probably met a new guy," I said.

"When she shows up, tell her we went home to eat supper," my mother said.

She leaned over and kissed me on the cheek. The smell of her perfume brought to mind all things safe. In that brief whiff of her scent I realized how much I missed home.

After they left, but not before a few tears were shed, I pulled the domed lid off my evening meal. No cheeseburger this time, but, even in my present state, I was hungry, and the grilled chicken, mashed potatoes, and peas—bland a dinner as it was—made me feel better. I piled my empty plate with the plastic wrapper from my utensils, the balled napkin, and empty milk carton, then replaced the domed cover and pushed the table away from me.

My pillow called. It must have been the bandage that made my head feel so heavy, for even as the weight of it landed on the pillow I experienced some relief. Some. A burden of a different sort lingered, weighing down my thoughts. It was as though I were balanced in a canoe, without paddles or flotation device, on a deep, dark ribbon of water, coursing one minute over immense rocks and coming the next face to face with boulders jutting from the river banks. On one bank, endless quicksand lurked, ready to suck me into its bowels and slowly suffocate the breath from me if I dared step on its shoreline. On the other bank, a tall, steep slippery wall of slate stood. Its own massive height cast a shadow over its face. I could see no visible way to pull myself to safety. Instinctively I knew this narrow ribbon of water would be joining a fast-running river and then, at a later point, dash over a powerful waterfall, plunging me to certain death. The only help available to me was the brain God had given me, and my desire to survive.

My eyelids grew heavy, and as I drifted off, I sensed the white eagle gripping my shoulders once again with its talons. I wondered where we would go this time.

I jerked awake. Silence wrapped me, like a blanket, heavy with meaning. I glanced around, searching for the white eagle. I was sitting, cross-legged on the ground. In front of me was the new fifteen-foot-tall, bronze statue of the white settler jumping from horseback to thrust his stake into the ground and claim his land. The canvas covering the centennial statue had blown off in the stiff wind whistling down Grand Avenue. Next to me, and continuing in a solid circle around the statue, several rows deep, were Poncas. Their peaceful protest observed by anyone driving past city hall; their silence punctuated every so often by an angry honk of disapproval.

"How long have you been here?" I asked the woman to my right.

She wore her long, black hair in a pair of braids. Her simple turquoise attire fitted loosely over her slim frame. Her eyes spoke of heartbreak, but she did not speak nor acknowledge that she had heard a word I'd said.

I glanced around at the solemn expressions of the protestors, the pensive attitude of a people who had known more than their share of despair and yet survived. They had flourished in the worst of conditions, devastating circumstances that would have rendered most any other people extinct. If the United States' government had moved them with the thinking that they wouldn't survive the trek, Uncle Sam had greatly underestimated the noble spirit of the Poncas. I peered to my left to find Chief White Eagle sitting beside me. We took in the vision.

"Two weeks," he said.

"They've been sitting here for two weeks?"

"Yes. Do you remember the story of the bear?"

"He stood alone. He learned to look inside himself."

Chief White Eagle's somber gaze met mine.

"Good."

"Like Standing Bear," I said, "these people are making a stand for what they believe is right, even if they have to sit to do it."

Chief White Eagle's eyes twinkled and his lips turned up slightly at the corner.

"You're being jocular."

Yet underlying his words I sensed pride. In me, perhaps?

"A bit, yes. Not to offend, though," I said quickly.

"No offense taken."

"How much longer will they sit here?"

"As long as it takes."

Suddenly a frail elder across the plaza slumped to one side; with haste, those around him fetched a ladle of water and pressed it to his lips. "They're fasting," said Chief White Eagle. "It is custom to fast during a mourning period. They mourn for those who have gone before them, for Crazy Arrow, and for Leslie Cries For War."

"Did Mr. Crazy Arrow die?"

"Yes."

"And Leslie?"

"He died a different death."

"Inside?"

"Yes."

A sadness washed over me, like salt poured in an open wound, absorbed into my flesh and bones, I shriveled. I felt weary. Old. I was too weak to speak, too forlorn to move from my self-dug grave. My spirit separated from my body. I could see my aged bones, the skin stretched thin across them, transparent and of little use.

"I'm too young to die!" I called out. "I'm too young to die!"

Someone jostled my shoulders, shouting, "Dusty, Dusty, wake up! Wake up Dusty!"

My eyes opened and Danielle was there, standing next to my bed.

"Am I alive?"

"Of course," she said, releasing her grip on me. "You were having a nightmare."

"What day is it?"

"It's Monday. I'm sorry I'm so late getting here. Practice ran over and . . ."

"You don't have to explain. I'm glad to see you."

"Me too. I'm glad you're okay." Her eyes took in my discolored face, the turban bandage, the plaster cast on my arm. "At least you're in one piece."

"I dreamt that I had died."

"Bummer. No wonder you were screaming."

"My head hurts again."

"Do you want me to like, get the nurse, or something?"

"Yeah."

Danielle strode out of the room, and I rested my head against the pillow. I wondered about Danielle sometimes. She hadn't picked up any of my mother's nurturing abilities. While other girls were babysitting to earn extra money and successfully socking away cash for their college fund, new clothes, or movie tickets, Danielle spent her time on hair and makeup to the point of obsession. And, of course, on boys. But to her boys were more a game of conquest, a notch on the proverbial belt. I'd never understood her. Genes are a real puzzle.

The burly nurse strode into my room all business; behind her Danielle made silly gestures. I found myself smiling, despite every effort to control the urge.

"May I have another pill?" I asked the nurse.

"It's a tad too soon," she said.

She smiled as if to soften the news. If I hadn't been lying down, I would have fallen over. Guess looks can be deceiving, I thought.

"I'll bring it in for you in thirty minutes. You'll probably be ready to go to sleep for the night by then, anyway."

She turned and walked out the door.

After she was out of earshot, I turned to Danielle.

"Are you trying to get me killed? That woman could have me for breakfast if she had the notion."

"Just trying to cheer you up, brother. I could really go for a pop. Want one?"

"Sure."

"I saw a pop machine in the waiting room down the hall."

Danielle bebopped out of the room, moving to some internal song. She returned, set a can down for me, and plopped herself into one of the two chairs. She put her feet up on the edge of my bed and leaned back, drawing long swallows from her soda.

"How's Jack?" I asked.

"Usual story. He doesn't want me to date anybody else, and we've only known each other a week."

"Shoot," I said. "I've known you to take longer than that to decide what to wear to go to the grocery store. Besides, Garret and I . . ."

"Garret and you what?"

"Aw, nothing. Never mind."

"I haven't seen Garret for awhile. What's he up to?"

"I don't know. We aren't . . . that good of friends."

"What? Since when?"

"Can we change the subject?"

"Sure." Danielle finished her pop and stood up to go. "I've got a ton of homework. And I haven't had a bite since lunch. I'll see you tomorrow, okay?"

"Yeah. Thanks for the pop."

"Yeah. Feel better."

I slumped back under the covers and laid my head against the pillow. *How could something that had been so soft, suddenly feel more like cement than foam rubber,* I wondered.

I closed my eyes just in time to see myself being swept downstream on the canoe again, faster and faster, the current bringing me ever nearer to the river that lay beyond. Time was ticking away. Every moment that went by increased the pain I was inflicting on others, injustice perpetrated solely by my own indecision.

TEN

I MUST HAVE FALLEN ASLEEP, for when I opened my eyes the room was dark, with only the light from the hallway illuminating the doorway. The door was ajar, and beams of light cast triangles on the floor and walls. I blinked the sleep from my eyes and realized I was not alone in the room.

Seated on a chair near my bed, his head thrown back and balanced against the wall, his legs stretched out in front and crossed at the ankles, my father slept. His mouth hung open, relaxed; he drew in slow, rhythmic breaths, his chest rising and falling. One arm draped over the armrest of the chair and dangled, the other lay in his lap.

I watched him for awhile. When did he come? Why? Why was he sleeping in a chair when he should be at the store? What time was it? I checked my wristwatch. Four o'clock. He would just be getting out of bed if he were home. I debated whether to wake him or not.

My father was one of those people who seemed to know how to handle every situation. I remember thinking as a child that he was like God. He never let me down. As I grew older I realized that most everybody sees their father that way. Strong. Able to leap tall buildings in a single bound, if required. I'd always wanted to be just like him.

And now I was a disappointment, a disgrace to the family. I had floated so long on top of the water, following the rise and fall of each swell in the current and ignoring the black clouds looming on the horizon that I was unprepared to deal with the threat of a storm. Bad weather had snuck up on me, sucked me into its center, and hurled me into foreign waters—deep, dark, tempestuous waters with quicksand on one side, slippery slate on the other, and a raging river and waterfall just around the bend.

My father startled, waking with an involuntary jerk. His head came up, his eyes opened, and, for that instant before he realized where he was, he appeared lost. He gazed about the room, ran his fingers through his hair, stood up, and stretched his arms above him.

"Morning," he said.

"How long have you been here?" I asked.

"I guess all night. I stopped by after supper last night, and you were asleep. I must have dozed off myself."

He shoved his shirttail back into his pants.

"I was debating whether or not to wake you," I said. "It's after four."

"Tom's covering for me this morning."

"I'm glad I didn't wake you, then."

Our conversation bordered on stilted, but I sensed my father had some reason for coming to see me. He seemed to be waiting for the right moment. I recalled the way he had abruptly changed the subject yesterday; I'd had the same ominous feeling then, too.

"Listen, Dusty," he said, pacing back and forth.

He came to my bedside and leaned against it.

"There's something I've been meaning to say to you."

"Me too," I said.

"Let me finish, now that I've started," he said, in a determined

91

way, as though if he were interrupted he might never get the words out. "I owe you an apology."

"For what?"

This was unbelievable. He owed me an apology?

"I never should have asked you to follow that Cries For War family around the store. I had no idea the boy would get drunk and do what he did to you."

I could see the glimmer of tears wrestling to free themselves from his eyes. His lower lip trembled. "I'd never intentionally put you in harm's way. You do believe that, don't you?"

The tears won, falling to his cheeks, running down to his chin, dropping onto his shirt. He didn't wait for me to respond.

"When you didn't come home Saturday night, it never occurred to me that anything like this could have happened. Then, when they called and said you'd been brought to the hospital by that . . . that Indian . . . your mother had to hold me back, I was so angry. I've never been so angry. I don't know what would have happened if I had run into him on the street that night."

He rubbed at the tears on his chin.

"All I could think of was being here with you," he said, "but when I saw you, black and blue and that horrible gash on your head, I became mad all over again. I could barely restrain myself."

His hands balled into fists and his eyes glowed with anger, as though he were reliving that thirst for revenge.

"No. You have it wrong," I said, before I could stop myself.

When he looked over at me with pain contorting his face, I knew there was no turning back. I had made my decision; everything had to come out now. I only hoped that my father wouldn't hate me for it.

"You didn't let me finish," he said. "I admit that I've been wrapped up in the store, and I've neglected you for too long."

"Wait!" I said, louder than I intended. "Leslie didn't do this to me—Garret did."

Emotion drained from my father's face. "What?"

"Garret beat me up and threw me in the ditch," I said again. "Leslie saved my life."

"That can't be," my father said.

He shook his head back and forth, unable to fathom it.

"It's the truth."

"But I thought you and Garret were friends."

"So did I." I started to cry.

"Oh my dear boy," he said, taking me in his arms. "What nightmare have you been through?"

I couldn't speak for a long while. Sobs of remorse and hurt took over. No sooner did I get myself under control, then they'd well up again. Through it all, my father held me, his own tears mingling with mine. Finally, I was able to speak. Once I began, the words tumbled out of my mouth as easily as marbles rolling out of a bag.

"It started Friday night at the Fun Zone," I said. "Garret, Jimmy, and I were playing pool. Garret was getting ready to make his last shot, and somebody shoved Stephen Crazy Arrow into him. He missed the shot and got furious at Stephen. Then Jenna stuck her nose in it and made a deal with Garret, that if he played her and won, he could do whatever he wanted to Stephen. But if she won, he had to forget it ever happened. Well, Jenna won. But you know Garret, he never forgets anything, especially if somebody makes him look the fool."

I told him the whole story, start to finish. From the firecrackers at the parade, to losing my bicycle, to driving Garret's Chevy, to the scene at Crazy Arrow's house, to me blacking out in the ditch.

"Leslie must have found me, just like he said, and brought me to the emergency room."

"This is unbelievable, Dusty."

My father was sitting in a chair now, gazing at me with an incredulous look on his face. He ran his fingers nervously through his hair.

"I didn't remember what had happened at first, Dad. I swear. My head felt mushy inside when I woke up, but when I read the article in the paper it all came back."

"What an ordeal," my father said. "What an ordeal."

He stood and began pacing back and forth across the room, shaking his head as if in disbelief.

"I blamed that boy and he had nothing to do with it."

"I know," I said. "And he's been arrested."

"This is a very serious situation."

"It's all I've thought about. Yesterday, when you talked about keeping my mind occupied . . ."

"Is that why you looked at me so funny?"

I nodded.

"I saw the newspaper on the bed," he said, "and I didn't know if you had read that article or not, but when you gave me that disturbing look, I just knew you blamed me for what happened. That's why I stayed here all night, in case you woke up. I just had to set things straight."

He crossed over to me and gave me a tight hug.

"I've decided to tell the police what happened." I blurted out.

"I see." He released his grip on me. "Everything?"

He looked at me as though we were discussing how much homework I'd turned in this week. I knew he was implying that to tell everything would be to admit my own part in it. From driving without proper supervision to leaving the scene of a crime and aiding and abetting a felon. *How many years would I get?* I wondered.

"Will you stay here with me?" A lump lodged in my throat at the thought of being carted off to prison.

"Of course."

The sun threw rosy rays across the room as it peeked above the horizon. Even with the bandage wrapping my skull, my head felt lighter than it had for the past twenty-four hours.

A nurse strolled into the room, took my wrist in her hand, felt for an artery, and asked, "So how are we this morning?"

"Much better," I said.

"Your breakfast should be arriving shortly," she said, jotting down my pulse rate on her clipboard and sticking a thermometer in

94

my mouth. She checked my cast to ensure it wasn't too tight.

"The swelling has gone down some. You should be able to move your fingers more."

I nodded, wiggling my fingers in confirmation.

"I need to get your blood pressure." She wrapped the blood pressure cuff around my arm, attached the pressure gauge, and pumped air into the cuff. Just when it felt like my arm would explode, she opened the valve to slowly release the air. She noted the result on her clipboard and removed the thermometer from my mouth.

"Normal." She jotted down my temperature by my other vital signs. "My shift ends at seven o'clock, but I'll see you tonight."

"Okay," I said.

The nurse swung the clipboard under her arm and left, leaving my dad and me alone.

"I'm going to see if I can't find a decent cup of coffee in this place," my father said. "I think your call can wait until after breakfast."

"You say that like it will be my last meal."

"No," he smiled. "You're doing the right thing. And I'm proud of you for it."

"You mean you don't hate me?"

"Hate you? Of course not. You're my son. How could I hate you?"

"Even after the dumb things I did?"

"We all make mistakes. The question is, have you learned from them? I say you have. But there's no avoiding the consequences."

"That's the tough part. What are people going to say about me? And Garret. We'll never be friends again."

"It boils down to choices. You have to decide how you're going to live your life. A constitution with yourself. Like as Americans, we live within the bounds of certain laws. Maybe you'll decide that you're going to tell the truth, no matter what, from now on. Then when a situation arises, you already know the right way to handle it.

95

That's just one example. There are many other issues you need to think about."

"Like treating people with respect?" I asked.

"Exactly. You can choose to help the old lady across the street or walk on by."

"I was thinking more about how we treat the Ponca people."

"That came out of left field," he said.

He cleared his throat, trying to disguise the surprise in his voice.

"I've just been thinking about it a lot."

The muscles in his jaw tensed.

"That's a touchy subject right now," he said. "I think I'll get that cup of coffee."

He left so abruptly, I wondered if I had said the wrong thing. What kind of world was it, when even my own father automatically blamed Leslie for what happened that night. My dad might regret having me follow the Cries For War family around the store, but if it wasn't me doing it, it would have been Tom or one of the other employees.

All my life I had always believed my father knew what was best. I'd also gone along with Garret—despite his hateful words and actions. Yet I knew now that how we treated people, like the Cries For Wars family, was a tender spot on the belly of the people of Ponca City as a whole.

If only my dad and Garret could see what I'd seen, I thought.

Maybe it would open their eyes.

Eleven

MY FATHER RETURNED WITH A cardboard tray loaded with food from the hospital cafeteria. "I thought I might eat with you," he said, striking the same neutral tone and wearing the same expression he used to greet new customers at the store.

"Great," I said.

I could never have imagined how much it would hurt to be treated like a stranger by my own father. We ate in silence. I was grateful good manners excused me from talking with my mouth full, though it had never stopped me before. I don't think my father noticed.

With breakfast cleared, there was nothing left to do but telephone the police. I made the call, and within fifteen minutes an officer, lean and sharply pressed, appeared to take my report. He phrased his questions carefully, trying not to upset me, but it didn't make the retelling any less painful.

Through it all, as promised, my father sat by my bed, offering me looks of support and comfort. As I retold once more the story of the stabbing, the officer's eyebrows raised slightly. I couldn't help wondering what he was thinking. When I was done, the officer's demeanor gave me no clue as to his mind-set. He was all official protocol.

"I need you to read this over and sign at the bottom," the officer said, matter-of-factly.

He turned to my father.

"You might want to stop by the barracks to see if you can identify Dusty's bicycle. If it's not there, check the pawnshops around town."

I read over the report. He had included every detail, written in cryptic, legalese that reduced the whole sordid mess to a dry, faceless bunch of facts. I signed on the bottom line.

"What's going to happen now?" I asked.

"From your testimony and Jimmy Joncas', the district attorney will probably issue a warrant for Garret Rogers' arrest."

The officer glanced at my father.

"Do you have an attorney?"

"We've never needed one before, not a criminal attorney, at least."

My mood dropped to an all time low. Criminal attorneys, warrants, testimonies. If I had kept my mouth shut it would have been much simpler. The police already had someone in custody. Now I'd implicated Jimmy, too. I knew his family couldn't afford to hire an attorney. He would end up with some appointed attorney and who knew what would happen to him. And Garret. He was only sixteen, but these were serious charges. Would he be charged as an adult? And what if Mr. Crazy Arrow died?

The scene of the Cries For War family huddled in their tiny kitchen from my dream popped into my mind. I could not explain to my father how I knew the hardships they had suffered or my reasons for speaking to the police. But I could not let my father blame himself for my stupidity. I recalled the story Chief White Eagle told of the buffalo: *A time to be quiet. I did not speak of what I had heard.*

A wise man speaks few words. I would have to accept my punishment. Go peacefully.

The officer reached for his back pocket and I held up my hands.

"I don't know if those cuff links will fit around my cast."

The officer's gaze met mine. Fighting the smile at the corners of his mouth, he pulled a ballpoint pen from his hip pocket.

"Well, I don't think you pose a threat to society in your condition, Dusty, unless you start wielding that plaster cast against the nurses."

My father chuckled, then turned quiet.

"Seriously, what do you think is going to happen?" my father asked the policeman.

The officer caught my father's eyes square on.

"That decision rests solely with the judge."

I realized from the officer's words that he wasn't about to second-guess the situation. I was filled with a sense of foreboding. Tears sprang from what appeared to be an overflowing cistern hidden behind my eyes. Would it ever dry up?

The police officer closed his notebook.

"Hope you're feeling better," he said, and he left us.

His absence didn't make me feel any better. If anything I wished he would have thrown me behind bars right then and there. At least in jail, I wouldn't have to face anyone. After awhile, everyone would forget where I was. My parents' lives could return to some semblance of what they had been before I screwed up.

"Dusty," my father said, jolting me out of my reverie. "I have to get over to the store. Keep your chin up, son. I know it might seem overwhelming right now, but, you'll see, it will work out in the end. You can't go wrong by doing the right thing."

He hugged me and with a sad backwards glance, he left.

I'd never felt so alone as I did at that moment. Doing the right thing was the easy part, it was the consequences of my actions that threatened to do me in. Stephen Crazy Arrow. How must he be feeling right now? The room was closing in on me. I needed to move around . . . Stephen Crazy Arrow . . . Stephen Crazy Arrow.

I jumped out of bed, slipped on my one-sleeved robe and my slippers, and walked out the door. What floor had ICU been on? One floor down, if memory served.

Holding onto the railing along the wall, I moved down the hallway until I located the elevator—stairs were out of the question given my lack of balance and fatigue. I rode one floor down, exited the elevator, turned right, and followed the signs to Intensive Care. The waiting room was empty. I went to the nurses' station and asked for Mr. Crazy Arrow's room number.

The same nurse who had attended to me while I was in the ICU looked up from a book she was reading.

"Here, I'll show you. You can only stay a few minutes."

She came out from behind the desk and walked ahead of me to a closed door. Swinging it open, she motioned me to enter.

I glanced inside, looking for Stephen. Mr. Crazy Arrow lay still on the bed; eyes closed. He was connected to every imaginable machine and monitor.

But no Stephen.

"How is he doing?" I asked.

"About the same," she said, without no hope in her voice.

"Where's Stephen?"

"His mother came and got him. She thought he needed some fresh air. He's been here since his father was brought in. The poor boy fell to pieces when it happened. Don't stay long. You need your rest, too."

She smiled at me as she said it; hers was a such a sad smile. I guess if I worked in such a place and saw so much death I would have a difficult time mustering a happy smile, too. I walked over to the chair Stephen had been sitting on in my dream and sat down.

As I watched Mr. Crazy Arrow breathe with the help of the respirator—oxygen tubes in his nose, all the monitors and wires, machines monitoring his vitals—I recalled the night that started it all. The madness and shock of it. Garret in a fit of rage as I'd never seen before. Mrs. Crazy Arrow running across the yard screaming, willing to risk her own life to save her husband's. Stephen staring at me from the window.

How could I face Stephen? I stood and hurried out of the room, suddenly afraid that he would return and catch me there.

What was I thinking? I made my way back to the elevator, up one floor, into the haven of my lonely hospital room. Who was I to think I could change the reality of that night by showing up out of the blue like that? Stephen had no reason to speak to me. What if it were my father who'd been attacked and was attached to all those machines, holding onto life by a thread? How would I feel? I'd want to beat the living life out of those responsible.

I climbed into bed and pulled the covers over me. My head hurt again, but I didn't want to take any more pills. I would only fall asleep and then I'd start dreaming. I didn't want to see anymore. I wished I wasn't all alone. I wanted to talk to someone, about anything, anything but the mess I'd made of my life . . . I wanted someone to help me stay awake.

School. The thought got me out of bed, and I picked up my notebook from the window ledge. It had come to this, forced to study to clear my head of everything else. I sat down on a chair and opened the notebook. Someone had clipped a list of assignments to the inside cover. Geometry ought to require most of my mental power, I thought. I grabbed the textbook, opened it to the assigned page, and began working the problems.

The next hour passed with me trying to understand the relationships of points, lines, angles, and surface shapes. It was far from my favorite subject, but doing my math homework kept me awake and my brain functioning at full power, leaving no space for recriminations to seep in.

A knock on the door finally broke my concentration. I lifted my pencil and raised my eyes to focus on the slowly opening door.

"Jenna!" I said. "Wow!"

She rushed towards me, arms outstretched; she tightly wrapped both arms around me, kissed each of my bruised cheeks, and then stepped back to look at me.

"You look absolutely hideous."

Her green eyes danced, as she made her pronouncement.

"I'm glad you're my friend," I said. "Imagine what my enemies will say when they see this face."

She took the schoolbooks from my lap, piled them on the window ledge, and plopped down on the chair next to me.

"So."

"So what?" I asked.

"So . . . tell me what happened."

She pulled one knee up and hooked it in the space between the arm rest and the seat, her body facing me. I could feel those green eyes assessing me. *Was that pity I saw in them?*

"You'll just say 'I told you so,' " I said.

"I promise I won't say that."

"You'll be thinking it though."

"I'll keep my mind open."

"How is it you always know the right thing to do?" I asked.

A smirk formed on her lips, but I saw the question in her eyes.

"I'm serious," I said.

"The problem with you, Dusty, is that you try to please everyone. I've seen it happen over and over. You do it with your parents, me—lots of times, and especially Garret. You let others think for you, persuade you. I can't remember a time when I've asked, 'What do you want to do?' and you were the one to decide."

"Yeah, but . . ."

I had no response. True to form, Jenna had called the shot.

"Yeah, but how do you . . ."

"Know the right thing to do?"

"Yes," I said.

"I feel it, inside. You know that little voice in your head?"

"Yes."

"I listen to it. If I feel uneasy about my decision or what I'm

102

planning to do about something, then I listen even harder."

"That's it? That's how you know?"

"Yes, pretty much. Are you going to tell me what happened now or not?"

"Yeah, but first, have you ever heard of Chief White Eagle?"

Jenna didn't speak for a few seconds. She couldn't—her mouth had dropped open and her eyes were big as saucers.

"What's wrong?" I asked.

"What's wrong? I can't believe what I'm hearing is what's wrong. I thought you weren't interested in Native Americans."

"Have you ever heard of him? It's a simple question."

"You, who grew up in Ponca City, three miles from *White Eagle*, which just happens to be the Ponca Indian Agency and what's left of the tribal reservation lands, you're asking me if I've ever heard of the Ponca's primary chief, the one for whom that same agency was named?"

She was right. I felt so dumb. I'd never made the connection before. It made perfect sense. So, had I been dreaming when I saw that white eagle flying over my head? Surely not. The first time I saw the white eagle I was walking to Jenna's house after school, the same day I found the rotten banana in my locker. But, then again, she hadn't seen or heard it that day. And I remembered seeing the eagle the night I blacked out, after Garret punched me and threw me in the ditch. I also remembered thinking Garret must have heard its screeching, because on his way back to his car he ducked and looked up and down the road. The eagle's cry sort of sounded like a siren, maybe that's why Garret looked. I don't know. It was all too weird.

"Dusty? Are you all right?" Jenna said.

I nodded. "I never made that connection before."

She shook her head back and forth in disbelief. "You people are too much," she said. "No wonder there is so much division between the whites and the Indians in this town. Oh, I almost forgot to tell you. The city council meeting has been set for Friday morning."

"City council meeting? For what?"

"To make a final decision about the statue. Remember? The protest?"

I nodded. Images of my body as shriveled as an old man's flashed by like photographs in a slideshow.

"I'm going," she said, "even if I have to cut class. I hear they're expecting so many people to attend that they've moved the meeting to the Poncan Theatre."

"Oh," I said.

"Don't force yourself to sound enthused," she said, sarcasm dripping from her words.

"I'm sorry. I've had a lot on my mind lately."

"I can see that," her gaze directed pointedly at my turban.

I ignored her comment and changed the subject.

"What else do you know about Chief White Eagle?"

"I know that he kept his native dress until the day he died."

"When was that?"

"I think it was in 1914. There's a monument to his memory near Marland on a high mound on land from the original reservation. The monument is fifteen feet tall and has a white stone eagle on top."

"You've been there?"

"Sure. Chief White Eagle had the confidence and respect of not only his tribe but also of the white man, because they knew he was a man of his word. He was very wise and always led his people towards peace."

"A peacemaker," I thought aloud.

"You could call him that," Jenna said. "Why all this sudden interest in Chief White Eagle?"

"Just curious, I guess."

The buffalo. A wise man speaks few words.

"You're acting strange, Dusty Hamilton," said Jenna. She stood and faced me. "My lunch period is almost over. I've got to go."

"Okay."

"You didn't tell me what happened to you," she said.

"I will but not yet. I have a few things to work out."

"Weird," she said, turning and striding out the door.

I wasn't trying to alienate Jenna, but I knew that if I told her what Garret had done, she would not hesitate to tell me what I should do. She had said, and rightly so, that I let others think for me.

Her words had hit a nerve.

Like the bear, this time, I had to stand alone, look inside myself.

The sun changed position on my imaginary slate wall, erasing the shadows. I could not see any hand holds screwed into the side. I grabbed a tree limb floating on the fast current and began paddling towards the opposite bank.

Twelve

BEFORE I KNEW IT, I HAD RACED out of my room, down the hall to the elevator, down one floor. I didn't know what I was going to say to Stephen, but I had to go see him. I couldn't let him continue to blame himself for what had happened that night.

I went straight to Mr. Crazy Arrow's room, knocked lightly on the door, and pushed it open. Stephen was sitting in the chair closest to his father. He looked up at me as I came in, averted his eyes, stared blankly at the bed, where his father slept. His intertwined fingers tightened a little, giving me a clue to his state of mind.

I stepped inside the dimly lit room and crossed the distance between us.

"I wanted to say . . . how sad I am about what happened to your father." I'd said it. I didn't think I could.

"I wanted you to know that I told the police everything. Garret was wrong to treat you that way . . . I was wrong to let him. And if I can do anything for you, well, uh, I'm upstairs in Room 208. I wouldn't blame you if you never forgave me. But I am sorry."

I turned to leave, stepping slowly on tiptoe so as not to disturb either father or son. I couldn't blame Stephen for not speaking to me. I'm not even sure if he'd heard me, for he hadn't moved at all. I opened the door and started out, sneaking one last glance behind me. Stephen had dropped his head into his hands. Tears pricked at the corners of my eyes.

Without another thought, I turned around and went back into the room, pulled the door closed, and sat down on the chair next to him. He sobbed silently for a long while. Tears streamed down my own face, unchecked.

We sat side by side, without speaking for a long time, keeping vigil over his father, together. Sitting there was like being in a time capsule. The hours passed without notice, with no outward signs that day had turned to night. I couldn't hear the rush hour traffic from this inner sanctum, nor smell food cooking to signal dinnertime. The occasional nurse entering at regular intervals to chart any progress and exiting again on her pillow soft soles was our only measure of passing time.

Somewhere in the space between the nurses' rounds, Stephen and I started talking, if you could call it that. At first it was limited to little comments here and there about the nurses, then short exchanges about food and what we were craving that couldn't be had from the hospital cafeteria or vending machines. Pizza, for instance, not the type with the cardboard crust, but the kind with the thick, chewy, lumpy crust.

We found common ground in our favorite pizza crust.

From there, we discovered other areas in which our tastes overlapped. It was a start.

Every given chance, I would sneak out of my room and join him in ICU. And before long, we became inseparable. We ate meals together and helped each other with homework assignments. He explained the Indian ways and I shared stories of my family and our traditions. He told me of his plans to go to law school and I told him of my plans to do anything that did not require geometry. Stephen was the only one I told about Chief White Eagle and my dreams. And right there in that tiny room with the monitors blinking and the sound of oxygen being fed through tubes, and his father in a coma, I began to understand the true meaning of friendship.

For two days I stayed with Stephen, parting late in the evenings when I went back upstairs to my bed to sleep and he retired on two chairs pulled together and covered with a blanket in his father's hospital room.

Thursday night I had returned to my room late and climbed into bed, pulled the covers over me, laid back against the pillow, and closed my eyes, when I heard people in the hallway outside my room. I listened a little harder and recognized my parents' voices. They were in the midst of a hushed discussion that bordered on heated. I slid out of bed and crept closer to the door.

"I'm not going to be the one," my mother said. "If you want him to stay away from Stephen, you'll have to be the one to tell him."

"I don't want to hurt the boy anymore than you do," my father said. "It has to do with economics. What do you suggest?"

"I suggest that you ignore the mean-spirited people in this town who have nothing to do but gossip and cause trouble."

"But those people are our livelihood. I can't ignore it when a good customer, like Mrs. Pendergrass, takes her business down the street."

"Any decent person can see that Dusty did what was right. How could he do anything else?"

"Yes, but does he have to spend every waking moment with that Indian boy? I feel badly for Stephen, too, but you know his friendship can't lead anywhere but to trouble for them both. And we don't need anymore of that."

I hurried back to my bed and pulled the covers up over my head, shaking with anger. When my parents finally came into my room, I kept my eyes closed and pretended to be sleeping. I let them think the medication had sedated me. Even when my father touched my shoulder, I lay still—my eyes sealed closed, as though I were in a deep sleep.

When I was certain they had left, I threw off the covers and pounded my fist on the bed, until the muscles in my arm quivered and throbbed.

THIRTEEN

THE NEXT MORNING DAWNED without my having enjoyed a moment of sleep all night. Jenna had agreed to pick me up at eight-thirty and take me with her to the city council meeting. I cleaned up as much as I could and struggled into the clothes my mother had brought me earlier in the week. It was not an easy task with one arm out of commission.

Jenna arrived a few minutes late, delayed by a garbage truck blocking the entrance to a nearby street. We snuck out of the hospital by way of the stairs. My balance was much better than a few days ago, but if I needed it, I had Jenna to lean on.

The morning sun shone brightly; a light dew danced on the tips of the grass, as yet untouched by its rays. I hadn't been outdoors for nearly a week, and the fresh air raised my spirits and boosted my confidence for the task ahead. Or it did until Jenna pulled the car into a parking space opposite the Poncan Theatre.

"We're here," I said.

"You ready?" She asked, as she gave me a good hard look.

"Thought I was, but not I'm not so sure I can even make it from the car to the front door."

"Don't worry—I've got your back," Jenna promised.

"Famous last words."

She helped me out of the car, and we inched our way down the sidewalk (I was weaker than I realized). Finally, we reached our destination and pushed open the glass front doors of the historic theater. A mob of people were ahead of us, so it took a bit of being pushed and shoved about before we made our way inside to the meeting area. The place was packed wall to wall with people. We stood in the back, waiting for the mayor to call the meeting to order.

I glanced around the inside of the newly restored theater. The high ceiling was painted burgundy with gold trim. Heavy burgundy velvet curtains provided a backdrop for the city council members seated on chairs near the front of the stage. A podium and microphone sat square in the middle of the row of council members' chairs. As for the audience, it was a mix of people: Native Americans (both Ponca and from other local tribes), whites, Hispanics, children, old people, and other high school students who had obviously cut class to be here. A dull roar of voices filled the room.

The mayor, a slightly built woman with gray hair, called the meeting to order with a slap of her gavel. I bided my time, waiting patiently through the introductions of the city council members and the formalities that go with a town meeting such as this.

"This meeting is an opportunity for the people of Ponca City to come to a democratic decision about the inscription on the statue in question," the mayor announced to the room.

Because the people in the audience would not quiet down, it was difficult to hear anything the mayor had to say. Several times she stopped talking and pounded the gavel, but the angry rumble of voices persisted. It was time to act. I pushed my way through the angry crowd, ignoring the pointed jibes and comments as I passed my fellow citizens. As I climbed the steps to the stage, my heart raced with fear, and, for a moment, I was tempted to retrace my

111

steps and slip away into the crowd. But then I thought of Stephen and his father and the Cries For War family and all the Poncas who had suffered so much to make this land their home, and I knew giving up wasn't an option.

I strode to the podium in the middle of the stage and faced the audience. Unexpectedly the crowd quieted at the sight of me.

"I'd like to say something," I said to the lady mayor.

She nodded and stepped away from the microphone.

I drew in a long breath, relaxed my shoulders, and adjusted the microphone to my height.

"My name is Dusty Hamilton. I know I'm just a kid, but I hope that you'll listen to what I have to say. I love Ponca City as much as anyone. I've lived here my whole life, and I'm proud to be a citizen of this town. My parents take great pride in telling about when their grandparents came to Oklahoma from England to stake their claim. I'm sure each of you can tell similar stories. We are proud of our heritage. That's what the celebration last weekend was all about.

"But the Ponca people, and the Sioux, and the Cherokee, and the Seminole, they were the first Americans. They came from Nebraska, Virginia, Florida, California, Arizona, before they were states. Not England, not Germany, not Italy, not Poland. For thousands of years the Indian peoples have lived on the land that stretches from the Pacific to the Atlantic oceans. Before it was America. Before it was the United States of America.

"When the pilgrims were starving, it was the Indians who shared their food. And we thanked them by pushing them off their land, herding them as if they were cattle away from their homes, their farms, their burial grounds. We tried to make them into one people, stripped them of their beliefs, insisted they live like us, look like us.

"The Poncas did their best to live alongside us in Nebraska as good neighbors. The Ponca never raised a weapon against our country; they learned to farm and build houses. Many of them learned English. And still, when it was in our own selfish interest, we took their land again and forced them to walk hundreds of miles to a

112

place so different from their northern homelands that they didn't know what crops to grow or what plants to use for medicine.

"And still, once again, they adapted to what our country asked of them. All they asked in return was that we not forget the sacrifices they made to get here. All they asked was that we recognize their history is also American history.

"Now they ask that we consider their feelings before we act yet again in our own selfish interests—before we forget that there are two sides to the story of how this land was settled. And how do we respond? We close our ears. They don't want to take our land, like we've done to them, over and over. They only want to be treated as human beings. They only want a little respect.

"Why does the statue need an inscription? Didn't the artist create it to speak for itself? Why do we need to add words that serve only to hurt our neighbors?"

The audience sat in stunned silence. At first I thought they'd gotten up and left, it was so quiet. Then, from the back of the theater I heard someone begin to applaud. I squinted my eyes to see who it was, smiling when I recognized the man clapping. It was my father. Others joined in, and soon the theater was filled with applause and hoots of good cheer.

I ran across the stage, down the steps, up the aisle. Folks moved aside to let me pass. My father raced down the aisle towards me, arms outstretched. He swooped me up in his arms, and we held on to each other, as though nothing would ever separate us again.

FOURTEEN

THE PONTOON BOAT DRIFTED aimlessly on Kaw Lake. The sun, high in the wide cloudless sky but so bright that its rays warmed my skin through my shirt. A gray heron cruised on the gentle wind just above the water, before determinedly diving into the lake. When it rose from the water, it did so as victor, grasping a thrashing fish that would be its next meal.

Stephen sat with his feet propped up on the bait box, his fishing line cast far out in the deep blue water. His forehead showed no signs of the furors that had crisscrossed it during that difficult week after his father died. I knew the pain and loss was still with him, but he'd found a way to carry on.

My father had dropped anchor and now slept in a lawn chair on deck. Nothing disturbed the peaceful calm surrounding us.

Stephen and I had long ago lost the need to talk nonstop. Listening to the wind, hearing the song of the water lapping against the boat was conversation enough for the both of us.

I remembered Chief White Eagle's story of the mouse. Floating in the middle of acres of water, I knew what it was to be insignificant. I'd learned to take comfort in simple pleasures.

The quiet was broken by the sound of screeching far off in the distance. The great white eagle grew louder as it approached, tightening its circle, drawing near. I was no longer afraid of him. He, too, had become a friend.

My heart quickened with anticipation as the great bird circled close above the boat, his wise golden eyes peered down at me, as he kept aloft with the slightest flick of his wings. He screamed once more and then soared up, high into the sky and out of sight. I wondered when, or if, I would see him again.

Stephen leaned over and picked up something from the bottom of the boat.

"A white eagle feather," he said.

I could hear the reverence in his voice.

He held the feather up towards the sky.

"My friend, only the most courageous warriors receive these."

He held the feather out to me.

"Dusty White Eagle Feather, through your courage you have earned this."

I took the feather from him and smoothed the velvet hairs between my fingers.

"The bear taught me strength," I said. "The buffalo taught me to be wise. The mouse taught me humility. The eagle gave me vision.

"But most importantly, Stephen, you have taught me the true meaning of friendship and how to forgive."

EPILOGUE

I SLAMMED CLOSE MY locker door. The noise echoed through the empty hallway. Today was the last day of the summer break. Tomorrow, the halls would be full of students. This year, my third year as a math teacher at Ponca High School, promised to be great. I know I always swore I would never do anything that involved geometry, but once I discovered the secret to playing pool was directly related to the principles of angles taught in that branch of mathematics, my attitude about the subject changed and it was a breeze to master the language of geometry.

I walked down the hall, out the front door to the top of the cement steps. I gazed down the brick street and across to Jenna's old house. Memories rolled through my mind like a filmstrip. I tried to recall the last time I'd seen Jenna.

After our high school graduation, she had gone off to college to study anthropology, to satisfy her longing to understand the origins of man. She was married now. She and her husband, Leslie Cries For War, and their baby daughter, Glory, were said to be back home between art shows. Leslie, it seems, had a talent and a passion for painting—watercolors, to be exact. Beautiful studies in moody shades, depicting scenes of the old Indian ways.

I remembered now when I'd last seen Jenna, it was the summer before last. We had spent an evening barbecuing, listening to country music, and dreaming about the future.

Jenna and Leslie were off to an art show in Santa Fe after that. Jenna planned to travel with Leslie as much as she could until the baby began school. By that time, they hoped, he could open his own studio somewhere, and they could settle down as a family. Buy a little house, maybe.

As for me, I had never forgotten the lessons Chief White Eagle taught me. Nor the pain of my mistakes. I paid for those mistakes through hours and hours of community service at the Ponca Indian Child Welfare office and the local soup kitchen. I even spent time cleaning up litter on the highways leading into Ponca City.

Jimmy received a similar punishment, but his service hours were spent cleaning the fire station and the firefighters' equipment.

My learner's permit was also revoked for one year. Luckily, someone had turned in my bicycle to the police, so I wasn't without transportation, primitive as it may have been for a high school senior.

I guess we learned something from our penance. Jimmy became a fireman after high school. I became the kind of teacher who doesn't judge a student by the color of his skin. I sometimes see Jimmy sitting on a lawn chair in front of the fire station, waiting for a call to come in from someone who needs help. We're not as close as we once were, but I like to think we're still friends.

Every now and then I think of Garret. Since his release from the juvenile detention center, he's been in and out of prison, mostly on minor charges. I often wonder what it will take to make him change. I guess some people never do.

Armed with a teacher's steady paycheck, I found a little fixer-upper in town and I'm remodeling it on the weekends. Still single. No real ties. Except for my students. And my family.

Danielle opened her own beauty shop in the new strip mall. Stephanie starts eighth grade tomorrow. My mother decided to go back to college and finish her degree in accounting. She plans to work with my father at the grocery.

Since several new industries have moved into town, business has picked up again at the store, and my father has hired a new assistant manager. We go fishing every chance we get.

As far as relations between the Poncas and the townspeople, it's better. The lines of communication have opened up, and I sense the beginnings of change. South of town a park has been established in honor of Chief Standing Bear, and every year it seems more people attend the tribal powwow and join in other traditional Native American cultural events and celebrations.

Come to find out, more folks around these parts have Ponca blood in their family trees than they knew. And even Poncas are researching their own familial connections with the other surrounding tribes, the Kaw, the Tonkawa, the Otoe-Missouria, the Osage, and the Pawnee.

"Hey, Dusty White Eagle Feather!" hollered Stephen, as he strolled up the sidewalk towards me.

He no longer wears his hair in two braids but in a ponytail down his back. He cuts quite a dignified figure in his navy suit and tie.

I two-stepped it down to meet him.

"Where should we eat, counselor?" I asked.

"I'm in the mood for pizza," Stephen said.

"Thick and chewy crust."

"The lumpier the better."

He slapped me on the back and we climbed into my car.

AFTERWORD

ONE PERSON CAN MAKE A difference. In this case, it was Edward Pensoneau, an elder of the Ponca tribe. In 1993, after the uproar about the wording to be inscribed on the centennial land run statue subsided, the Ponca City fathers and mothers went looking for a way to recognize the contributions and suffering endured by Native Americans, including the local Ponca.

In that spirit, Edward Pensoneau wrote a letter to the tribal council suggesting that Chief Standing Bear, one of the five Ponca chiefs at the time of the tribe's relocation from Nebraska to Oklahoma, be honored.

His idea at first met with opposition.

Some thought any statue erected in Ponca City should be of Chief White Eagle, since he was not only the tribe's main chief at the time of the relocation to Oklahoma Territory but also the chief who remained there with his people after Chief Standing Bear and his small contingent returned to the tribe's old lands by the Niobrara River.

Others agreed with Pensoneau.

Consensus came after Pensoneau reminded everyone that while Chief White Eagle was—and would always be—an important local hero, Chief Standing Bear's testimony on behalf of all Native Americans—testimony that led to Native Americans being recognized as "persons" under the law in the eyes of the American government and, thus, free to enjoy the rights of any other person in the land—made him one of our country's most important historic figures . . . and one of the country's first civil rights activists.

Pensoneau's words resonated with both Poncas and non-Native Americans and with other local tribes, and they proved to be the salve needed to advance the community's healing.

In 1996, a twenty-two-foot tall, bronze statue of Chief Standing Bear, by artist Oreland C. Joe, was erected on a small rise south of Ponca City. The statue was faced east to the rising sun to symbolize new beginnings.

For almost a decade, the statue stood alone in rustic surroundings—the tall grass of the prairie rising to its very edge.

Then in 2007, it got the home it deserved. The sixty-three-acre Standing Bear Native American Park also saw the opening of the Standing Bear Museum and Education Center.

The building of that center was accompanied by improvements in how Chief Standing Bear's statue was displayed.

Today, a plaza contains the inlaid names of the eight clans of the Ponca Tribe radiating out in a circle from the foot of the statue. Nearby large sandstone boulders surround the parameter, each bearing the official brass seal of one of the six tribes that makes their home in northern Oklahoma: the Osage, the Pawnee, the Otoe-Missouria, the Kaw, the Tonkawa, and the Ponca.

The park draws locals, tribal members, and tourists.

And every year, on the last weekend of September, a powwow in honor of Standing Bear is held at the park. The whole town turns out for the powwow, as well as non-Native people from across the state. Native Americans from across the country come to share in

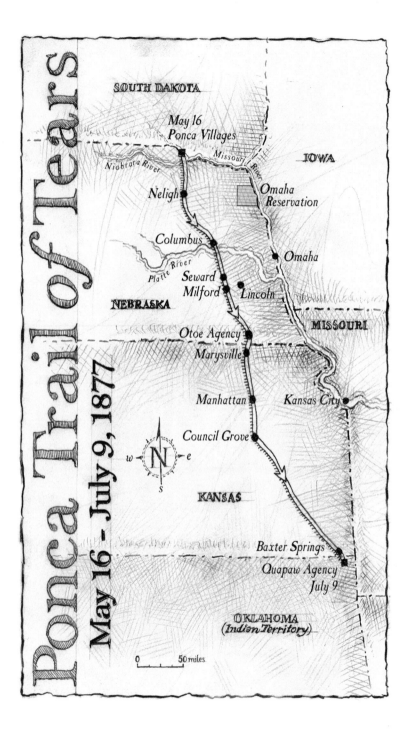

Ponca Trail of Tears

May 16 – July 9, 1877

SOUTH DAKOTA

May 16
Ponca Villages

Niobrara River

Missouri River

IOWA

Nelgih

Omaha
Reservation

Columbus

Platte River

Omaha

Seward
Milford

Lincoln

NEBRASKA

MISSOURI

Otoe Agency

Marysville

Manhattan

Kansas City

Council Grove

N
w   e
s

KANSAS

Baxter Springs

Quapaw Agency
July 9

OKLAHOMA
(Indian Territory)

0   50 miles

the celebration, to compete in the dance competition, and to exhibit traditional crafts and foods.

In the end, Edward Pensoneau's suggestion has led to not only recognition for Chief Standing Bear but also a deeper understanding and appreciation of Native ways—and the realization that many tribes experienced their own Trails of Tears during the relocation years.

The healing could never have happened, however, without the interest, willingness, and cooperation of all those concerned: the people of Ponca City and the six local tribes—the Ponca, the Kaw, the Tonkawa, the Otoe-Missouria, the Pawnee, and the Osage.

And it could never have begun had Chief Standing Bear not in 1879 had the courage to stand in a courtroom before the world and declare:

"I am a man. The same God made us both."

About the Author

Lesson of the White Eagle is Barbara Hay's debut young adult novel. Her work has appeared in the Tulsa World, *Columbia* magazine, the Sooner Catholic, and *Women's World Weekly*. Hay holds a bachelor's degree in liberal studies from the University of Oklahoma. The widowed mother of four children, she lives and writes at her home in Ponca City, Oklahoma. Visit her at www.BarbaraHay.com.

QUESTIONS FOR DISCUSSION

1. How does the title of *Lesson of the White Eagle* relate to the story?

2. How believable were the characters? Which character do you identify with? Why?

3. Is the protagonist sympathetic or unsympathetic? Why? If not, what would make him someone you could emphathize with?

4. What themes—friendship, racism, bullying, family—recur throughout the book? How does the author use and develop these themes? Do they work?

5. Why do certain characters act the way they do? What motivates Dusty Hamilton to do something that he would not normally do? Why does Dusty make excuses for Garret? Is there anything you would call "out of character"? Does the character grow over the course of the story?

6. What types of symbolism are used in this novel? What do these objects represent? How do characters react to and with these symbolic objects? What objects carry symbolism in your own life?

7. Discuss the broader social issues that this book tries to address. Does the author believe different racial groups can coexist in a community? How are the two cultures—the Ponca people and non-Natives—portrayed in the book? Fairly? Unfairly? Favorably? Unfavorably?

8. Where could the story go from here? What do you see as the future of these characters? What would our lives be like if we lived in this story? Do you believe the community is portrayed as it actually exists? Could communities like it exist in other parts of the country?

9. What is the character Chief Standing Bear trying to convey when he says, "My hand is not the color of yours, but if I pierce it, I shall feel pain. If you pierce yours, you also feel pain. The blood that will flow from mine will be the same color as yours. I am a man. The same God made us both." Who does he hope to convince? And of what?

10. How does the arrangement of the book help or detract from the ideas in the novel? How is the book structured? Flashbacks? Visions? From one or multiple points of view? Why do you think the author

chose to write the book this way? What did she gain by doing so?

11. Does the book fit into or fight against a literary genre? How does the author use tragedy to serve her story? Does this book typify a regional southwestern or western novel? If so, how?

12. How does this book relate to other books you have read? The book is described as a novel for young adults, but could you see it appealing to other ages, too? If so, would you recommend it for older or younger readers? Would you read another book by this author or recommend another of her books to someone else to read?

13. Is the setting of the book important to the story? Why or why not? How realistic is the setting? How does the setting differ from towns in your state or region?

14. What was the author's objective with this book? Do you believe she was successful?

15. What would you say is the author's world view?

16. What is the great strength—or the most noticeable weakness—of the book?

17. Do you believe childhood friendships differ from ones made in adulthood? What are the strengths

and weaknesses of childhood friendships?

18. Do you think most teens in Dusty's position would know how to go about ending a friendship with a strong personality, such as Garret? Would you?

19. Given what we know about Dusty Hamilton's upbringing, how could his ignorance about Native Americans be explained? Does his ignorance detract from him as a character? As the story develops, does Dusty become a more sympathetic character?

20. Why would a newcomer to Ponca City, like Jenna, possibly have a different perspective on Native Americans, than say Dusty, who has grown up in a state with 38 tribes.

21. Did this book change your views about Native Americans or Native American history? If so, how?

22. This story was set in the early 1990s, do you believe the issue of racism against Native Americans still exists? When you think of minority groups in the United States, do you think of Native Americans as one? Do you think racism against Native Americans garners the same attention that racism against other minority groups does?

23. In the story, Dusty's father has issues with Ponca people who shop in his grocery store. Could that explain Dusty's views? Does it excuse them?

24. How do you think treatment of Native Americans differs in small towns versus big cities, in western versus eastern states, in the north versus the south?

25. What did you like best about this story? What did you like least? What will you take away from this book?